ACQUIRED CHARACTERISTICS

by George A. Platz

Blue Lake Press

BLUE LAKE PRESS
A Western Division Subsidiary of the
Chicago, Whitewater & Mad River Company
P O Box 797, Blue Lake, CA 95525

ISBN: 978-0615464589

ACQUIRED CHARACTERISTICS

"I have hitherto sometimes spoken as if the variations--so common and multiform in organic beings under domestication, and in a lesser degree in those in a state of nature--had been due to chance. This, of course, is a wholly incorrect expression, but it serves to acknowledge plainly our ignorance of the cause of each particular variation. Some authors believe it to be as much the function of the reproductive system to produce individual differences, or very slight deviations of structure, as to make the child like its parents. But the much greater variability, as well as the greater frequency of monstrosities, under domestication or cultivation, than under nature, leads me to believe that deviations of structure are in some way due to the nature of the conditions of life, to which the parents and their more remote ancestors have been exposed during several generations."

--Charles Darwin, On The Origin Of Species (1859), p. 131

"The question is asked, What is the attitude of the Central Committee of the party to my report? I answer: The party's Central Committee examined my report and approved it."

--Trofim D. Lysenko, addressing the Lenin Academy of Agricultural Science, Moscow, August 7, 1948, at the conclusion of its week-long debate on genetics

1

"Comrade Walnik, this is good work. It won't be long until you're writing books for the capitalists to smuggle out to the West and making yourself a fortune." Leo Krakin put Walnik's smudged papers down on the table in front of them. A shock of thick, dark hair falling across his forehead made Krakin look younger than his thirty-eight years. The short, fat little man to whom he spoke--shorter even than Krakin's 170 centimeters--laughed. Krakin knew that the remark had struck home.

"Yes, while I'm dying in a labor camp for writing them." Walnik laughed again, coughed, and wheezed.

Krakin put his hand on Walnik's pudgy shoulder and gently directed the older man to the door of Krakin's apartment. "Now remember, not a word to anyone about the article. It will be hard when you actually see it in print, but if it gets out that you wrote it, we'll both wind up in a labor camp."

"You can count on me, Krakin." Walnik was now at the door, which Krakin had opened. "Well, good night," he said. "And good night to you, Comrade Malchev," he added, leaning around Krakin to speak to the girl in the room behind them. Krakin knew that Walnik couldn't resist one last look at Krakin's broad shouldered, big breasted, blond girlfriend. He turned around for a quick glance at her himself. Anya returned their looks with a smile.

Krakin started to close the door on his guest. "Good night, Comrade Walnik. See you again next Sunday."

Walnik went out to face the biting February wind that whistled down Basilgrad's narrow streets. Krakin shut the door and locked it.

"You're cruel, Leo," Anya said.

"Why? Because I use Walnik's article as my own? He doesn't care. You saw him. He's just tickled to get his writing in print."

"No, not that."

"Why, then?" Krakin sat down on the worn sofa next to Anya

and put his arm around her. She snuggled close to him.

"For making fun of his little dream. He thinks he can be another Tolstoy."

"Everyone in my writing group thinks he can be another Tolstoy. Only they don't care what they write about. They hope to pile up royalties in a Western bank account, so they can defect and live a luxurious, decadent Western life. That's what keeps them writing my articles for me."

"It's still not nice to make fun of their fantasies."

Krakin looked into Anya's wide-set blue eyes, now very close to his. She was serious. And she was probably right. "Perhaps I was a little thoughtless," he said.

"Not everyone is as cynical as you."

"Then how do they survive in this dreary socialist utopia?"

"Maybe the way that we do." Anya took Krakin's hand and looked up at him. "Did I ever tell you you have a very sensitive face?"

"Really?"

Krakin held her tight to him and felt the sensation of her soft, warm body next to his. He cherished his moments alone with Anya. They were a welcome refuge from the gray seriousness of the Soviet state nearly a decade after Stalin's death.

And they were all too few. An urgent pounding came from Krakin's door. He thought of ignoring it but couldn't. Anya was already pulling away and straightening out her dress. He got up and went to the door, irritated.

As soon as he opened it, a young man and woman pushed inside. The man appeared to be about twenty. He was heavy-set, though nowhere near as wide and muscular as Krakin, and straight, unkempt brown hair stuck out all over his head. The woman was tall and very thin and wore wire-rimmed glasses. She seemed about the same age as the man.

"Are you Leo Krakin?" the young man asked.

"Yes." Krakin needed a minute to size his visitors up before deciding how to deal with them. He had already concluded that they had to be University students.

"We understand that you . . . find things for people. For a fee," said the girl, in a rasping, unpleasant voice.

"You're wrong. I'm a journalist for the *Party Organ*. If you've lost something, see the police."

"You're very cautious, aren't you, Krakin," the man said. "Look, let's not fool around. We work for Professor Gregor Polokov at the University. I'm sure you've heard of him. And he knows about you. You were recommended by Director Balyuk at the University Museum. Polokov wants to hire you."

Krakin recalled the job he had about two years earlier recovering the gold pieces stolen from the Museum's collection. The Basilgrad police had received credit for the recovery, and very few people knew that Krakin had not only discovered the hiding place of the coins and tipped the Police Captain as to their location, but had also arranged it so that none of the coins found their way into the Captain's pocket. Balyuk did know, and therefore these kids were possibly on the level. But Krakin would have to have Anya check them out tomorrow. Her job at the Basilgrad University administration office gave her access to files on both students and faculty.

"Who are you?" Krakin asked.

"I'm Ilina Togorny," the girl answered. "This is Jan Kirus. We're students and laboratory assistants of Professor Polokov. He sent us to get you. He's rather in a hurry, if you don't mind. He must see you tonight." She spoke as if she thought a student of Professor Polokov commanded the same respect as an agent of the KGB. What gave kids these days such a sense of importance, Krakin wondered. Maybe they actually believed the Party slogans pasted on the University administration building: "Soviet Youth--Our Hope For Tomorrow."

"I can't possibly see Polokov tonight," Krakin said. "I've got to complete an article that goes to press tomorrow. I'll try to see him tomorrow if I can get away."

The girl gave a mocking laugh. "You're not working on any article. You're spending the evening shacking up with that cow over there." She nodded toward Anya, still on the sofa, who had been silently taking everything in.

Krakin exploded. The interruption was bad enough, but on top of that was the insolence and now the totally uncalled-for insult to Anya. He slapped the girl's face--not hard enough to damage anything, which he could have done easily, but hard enough to sting.

As Krakin had moved toward the girl the other student, Kirus, had slipped close behind Krakin. He now grabbed Krakin's arm and twisted it behind Krakin's back.

"All right, Krakin, we've asked you politely. If you don't come to see Polokov willingly, we'll just have to take you there."

"I've had about enough of this crap," Krakin responded. He slammed his free elbow into Kirus's breastbone. Kirus fell to the floor, gasping hoarsely.

The girl jumped at Krakin, but he took her wrist and twisted her around toward the door, then shoved her out into the hall, where she also fell to the floor. He grabbed Kirus by the collar and dragged him on his hands and knees to the door and pushed him out with the girl.

"You can't do this," screamed the girl.

"Who's going to stop me?" Krakin asked.

The girl glared at Krakin from the hallway, while her companion, obviously in pain, slowly rose to his feet.

"Oh, by the way," said Krakin. "Tell your Professor Polokov that I'll be at his office tomorrow morning at ten." He slammed the door on the two incredulous faces.

"Thank you for defending me from that woman," Anya said, still seated on the sofa. "You're so gallant."

Krakin grinned sheepishly. "I guess I lost my temper."

"What I don't understand is why after all that you agreed to see this Professor Polokov anyway."

"Isn't it obvious? It's because they didn't want me to."

Anya looked puzzled. "That isn't actually quite exactly how it appeared to me."

"If they had really wanted me, they would have behaved themselves better. No one who really wants help asks for it the way they did, not even University students. They probably have to go back and tell this Polokov that they asked me, and they wanted to say they tried as hard as they could and I refused."

"You're so brilliant."

"I want you to check both of them out for me tomorrow morning. Also Polokov. I'll stop by your office. But let's forget about them now. We've got better things to do."

2

Krakin scraped the frost off the inside of the second-story window and looked down into the square. Men and women bundled in heavy wool coats were hurrying to their jobs in the nearby government buildings. Across the square, white clouds of steam poured out of the chimneys of the Basilgrad Regional Central Committee headquarters and evaporated into the overcast morning gloom.

Krakin was the first to arrive at the *Party Organ* offices this morning. He wanted to be here when Ivan Sulka, the Chief Editor, came in. Sulka prized punctuality over everything else, and with good reason. The Central Committee rated him on his ability to get the magazine out on time. They didn't bother to read anything Sulka published other than the political drivel they themselves sent over to fill the first dozen pages of each issue.

Sulka's floppy fur hat appeared below, bustling toward the building entrance. Krakin picked up his folder and went to wait near Sulka's desk, behind a partition at the back of the large room. He heard Sulka clomping up the steps and across the wooden floor.

"Good morning, Ivan," Krakin said when the man was halfway across the room.

Sulka hadn't seen Krakin and started. He switched on the

lights.

"Oh, hello, Krakin. What are you doing down here so early?"

"I finished the piece on the cultural park last night, and I wanted you to have it right away, in case you decide to put it in next week's issue."

Sulka beamed. He had a round, peasant's face. A gold tooth highlighted his smile. "Let me see it. How long is it?"

Krakin handed Walnik's manuscript to Sulka. "About forty pages. You may want to cut it." Krakin knew that Sulka appreciated length, for the same reason he appreciated punctuality.

Sulka riffled through the pages. "Krakin, I don't know how you do it. This wasn't due until next week. I appreciate your effort."

"I can do it because I have a Chief Editor who understands how a journalist needs to work. If you had me sit in here at a desk all day, I wouldn't produce half as much."

Sulka patted Krakin on the shoulder. "We make a good team, Krakin. Anytime you want that Assistant Editor job, it's yours."

"Like I said, Ivan, that's not my kind of work. I'm better off where I am."

"It's your choice." Sulka took off his coat and hung it up. By now the other workers were starting to arrive. Krakin stayed near Sulka's desk.

"Was there something else, Krakin?"

"Yes. Have you ever heard of a professor at the University named Polokov? One of his students suggested him to me as a possible subject for an article."

"Never heard of him."

Krakin hesitated. "Do you . . . ah . . . think there might be anything on him in the Central Committee file?"

"I doubt it." Sulka sat down at his desk and began examining some papers. He looked up. Krakin was still there. "But if you want to take a look, I guess it wouldn't do any harm." He grinned at Krakin, his gold tooth gleaming. He fished through his pocket for a key, found it, and handed it to Krakin.

"Thanks, Ivan. I'll have it back in a few minutes."

Krakin went up to the third floor and down the corridor to a steel door at the back of the building. He unlocked it and went into the room beyond. Artkin, the clerk who kept the files, wasn't in yet. Krakin turned on the lights.

Among the tasks assigned to the staff of the *Party Organ* by the Central Committee was the keeping of these files. Every statement of opinion published in the magazine, or submitted to it, or uncovered by its writers, was supposed to be filed away here under the name of its author. The other government publications maintained similar files; rumor was that the *Red Banner*, the daily newspaper, had a whole floor devoted to such a purpose. Krakin himself had long ago stopped sending material to the files, an omission in which he took great pleasure.

Krakin searched through the card index to see if there was any record on his man. Sure enough, there was the card. Gregor Polokov, Professor of Biology, Basilgrad University. Krakin went to the cabinets, pulled open the appropriate drawer, and thumbed through the folders. They jumped from "Podzen" to "Pomerski." He looked through all the "Ps." No Polokov. Either the file was misplaced, or . . .

Krakin went back to the card index and took out the Polokov card. He turned it over and held it close to the light. A small "x" appeared in the lower left-hand corner. Krakin was one of the few who knew that this was Artkin's confidential indication that the file had been removed by the KGB.

3

Basilgrad University was founded and built by the Soviets in the 1920's, in the wake of the Revolution. Its older buildings, white and cement colored, reflect the proletarian monumental style of that time. The newer buildings, such as the Biological Sciences Building in which Professor Polokov's office was located, were simpler, less pretentious, and far less drafty structures of concrete and glass block. Krakin, after his walk from the tram stop half a kilometer away, appreciated the designers' attention to the thermal over the inspirational.

Like new universities everywhere, Basilgrad had a faculty that was mediocre at best. At least, thought Krakin as his prospective client greeted him in the second-floor hallway, Polokov made no pretense of looking like an eminent academician. He wore the tight-fitting imitation Western style clothes that had become so popular among Basilgrad's students. On the students they looked bad enough; on Polokov they looked ridiculous. He was a tall, extremely thin, gaunt man with sunken eyes and long, sparse brown hair. A glance into those wild eyes altered Krakin's initial impression: Polokov wasn't a peacock; he was a crackpot. Krakin had second thoughts about being there.

Polokov showed Krakin into a tiny office crammed with books and loose papers. Ilina Togorny and Jan Kirus, the two students who had visited Krakin the previous evening, were already there. They didn't get up when Krakin entered and returned his nod with hostile stares. Krakin had apparently not formed a lasting friendship in last night's encounter.

Polokov sat behind the desk and motioned Krakin to take the chair in front of him. He looked into Krakin's face for a moment before speaking. "How is it, Comrade Krakin," he said, "that you have time to investigate things? How do you manage to fulfill your plan? Doesn't the Labor Committee disapprove of this sort of thing?"

"I do my job. My other activities are my own affair. Now, what is it you want me to find for you?"

"A few more questions first." Polokov smiled condescendingly. "How much will I have to pay you?"

Krakin didn't like Polokov. He didn't particularly want to help him. "If I take the job, one hundred rubles a day. Three hundred minimum, in advance."

Polokov rubbed his chin and glanced at the two students. "Fifty a day."

"One hundred." Krakin started to get up.

"All right. One hundred. You pay your own expenses."

"In Basilgrad, yes. Outside, you pay."

"All right. What if you don't find it?"

Krakin shrugged.

"All right. All right. One more question. Will you keep everything I tell you absolutely confidential?"

"Yes, unless the law requires me to disclose it. Then I'll do as I'm required."

Polokov squirmed uncomfortably. "All right. Just don't volunteer anything."

Krakin nodded toward the two students. "What about them?"

"Oh, they're just as involved as I am. You can talk to them about it."

Krakin grinned at Kirus. The smile wasn't returned. Krakin looked again at Polokov. "Well, what is it I'm supposed to find?"

"A manuscript. It looks much like this." Polokov reached out his bony hand and picked up a brown-backed volume about eight centimeters thick, with pages of uneven length sticking out the bottom.

"What's it about?"

"Oh, descriptions of experiments. Theories. Hypotheses. I'm a biologist, Krakin. My field is genetics. The manuscript contains the results of my work for the past five years. It's my only copy. If only I'd made another."

"Any distinguishing marks?" Krakin pulled out the pad he always carried with him and scribbled a few notes.

"No. No title or anything. It doesn't even have my name on the cover. All of our names appear in it, of course, on the data sheets."

"Us?"

"Comrade Kirus, Comrade Togorny, and myself. They assisted in the experiments. That's why they're here."

"I see," said Krakin, writing. "Perhaps you should tell me a little more about the subject matter."

"It deals with, well, some inquiries into the process of evolution. How changes occur in organisms. This is all set out in the first pages."

"That ought to be enough to identify it. Why is it so important that I find it?"

"I told you. That manuscript is five years of my life. Perhaps that doesn't seem significant to you, but I am a scientist. My work is important. To lose five years . . ."

"I understand that," Krakin interrupted. "What I mean is, why do you want to hire me to find it? You scientists lose things all the time, but you don't bring someone in to investigate. Usually these things just turn up, under a bunsen burner or something. What's so different about your manuscript?"

Polokov looked at his students. They didn't say anything. Then he rose and stood in the narrow space between his chair and the wall. He held himself erect, his chest puffed out as far as possible, which wasn't far. "My manuscript is a major scientific document, Krakin. There are very few who know what I have been doing, but I will tell you, on your word not to reveal it."

"I told you that I wouldn't unless I have to."

"Yes." Polokov paused. "Tell me, Krakin, do you believe in the theory of evolution?"

Krakin shrugged. "I suppose."

"Of course you do. Evolution is the law of the land, as much as socialism. The Academy of Science tells us the laws of nature, just as the Central Committee tells us the civil laws. And of course the

Academy finds unacceptable any theory that suggests the existence of a God, or that is inconsistent with the principles of socialism. But I am not so bound." Polokov thumped his chest. Krakin feared he might break something, but he apparently didn't. He continued, "I have devised my own experiments. I have repeated the experiments published by the Academy. Their conclusions are wrong, Krakin, and I have proved it." Polokov was excited. His eyes flashed. "Tell me, Krakin, what do you know of the processes of evolution?"

"Natural selection. Survival of the fittest."

"Yes, that's one of them. What are the others?"

Krakin spread his hands. He didn't like being treated as a student.

"Natural selection by itself, Krakin, isn't enough. Natural selection by itself can operate on an organism for a billion years without producing a new species. The organism has to change *first*, before natural selection operates to produce evolution. Do you follow me?"

Krakin nodded. Polokov now started to pace back and forth in the narrow space behind his desk.

"What is it that causes organisms to change then? This is the crucial question. Darwin himself didn't know. The biologists of the West, Krakin, attribute change solely to spontaneous mutation of the genes. But does that occur frequently enough to cause an amoeba to evolve into a man? And what causes mutation to begin with? The Academy finds the Western theories inadequate. The Academy holds that changes in organisms are caused by adaptation to their environment, and that these changes are inheritable. The inheritance of acquired characteristics, they call it. This is not a new theory, Krakin. It pre-dates Darwin. But the Academy claims to have *proved* it. However, *my* experiments show the contrary."

Krakin was slightly bored. His evaluation of Polokov had not been changed by the man's raving. "Why are you telling me all this?"

"Because you asked why I have called on you to find my manuscript. You see, my conclusions challenge the official doctrines of the Academy of Science. If the document falls into the wrong hands, it could be very damaging to all our careers. I don't care about my reputation, but I don't want to lose my laboratory. I need it to finish my work. And it would be very unfair for my students to have their careers destroyed before they are begun." Polokov stopped.

Concern over the future of the two insolent kids sitting next to him didn't exactly move Krakin. He doubted that it really moved Polokov much either. "I still don't see why you need me," Krakin said.

Polokov sat down and caught his breath. "There is another reason also, Krakin. I don't think the manuscript was misplaced, as you have suggested. I think it was taken."

"What makes you think that?"

"I always kept the manuscript right here." Polokov patted the only empty space on the bookshelf beside his desk. "I know I'm not a neat person. I suppose you can see that by my office. But I was careful about the manuscript. I always put it right here when I finished going over it."

"When did you last see it?"

"Two days ago. Saturday. I worked on it, making revisions, until about eight o'clock in the evening, then I put it back on the shelf. Yesterday evening when I came in it was gone."

"Maybe your assistants used it after that." Krakin looked at Kirus and Togorny.

"Don't you think he's asked us about that?" said the girl nastily. "Do you think he would have called for you if Jan or I knew where the book was? I haven't seen the thing for over a week."

"Nor have I," added Kirus.

"You both know what's in it?"

"Of course," the girl answered.

Krakin looked at Polokov. "Who else would have had access to it?"

Polokov shrugged. "Anyone. The doors of my office aren't locked. The University doesn't permit it. The building is open. Anyone who knew about the book could have come in and taken it."

"Then who knew about the manuscript?"

"Other than these two," Polokov waved at the two students, "I don't know. I never told anyone about the manuscript. I've mentioned my work occasionally to people in my department, but I haven't discussed my conclusions." He paused and tugged at his collar. "There is one other possibility. Last fall Comrade Lysenko came here to give a speech to the students. Afterward, the faculty gave a reception for him. I was there. I drank a lot of vodka. I remember cornering Lysenko and talking to him at some length. I don't remember exactly what I said, but I may have mentioned my experiments and my manuscript."

"Who is Lysenko?"

"You've not heard of T. D. Lysenko?"

"The name does sound familiar, but I can't place him."

"Why, he's the President of the Lenin Academy of Agricultural Science and Director of the Institute of Genetics of the Academy of Science. It's his experiments that I've disproved." Polokov looked down and shook his head. "I may have told him everything." He looked up. "You see, he's wrong. He's absolutely wrong. I wanted him to know."

"You think Lysenko could have taken the manuscript? That seems rather far-fetched, doesn't it?"

"I don't know. He's a vain man and a powerful man. He has the personal favor of Premier Krushchev. I don't know that he would take my manuscript, but he might have informed the Academy, or the KGB."

"Is this something that would involve the KGB?" Krakin wasn't bored any longer.

"Some might think that my theories are inconsistent with the tenets of socialism, and therefore contrary to the interests of the State. Lysenko has used the KGB to force others who disagreed with him to recant. I believe there are many biologists in the U.S.S.R. who still disagree but are afraid to say so because of the KGB."

Krakin considered. "Professor," he finally said, "if the KGB is involved in this, I'm not. If they have your manuscript, I can't get it back, and I'll get sent to a labor camp if I try."

"But maybe it was Lysenko alone. Or someone else. Please, Krakin, won't you just look into it far enough to find out if it was the

KGB? I'll pay your fee. Here." He pulled out a wallet from his desk drawer. "Here's your three hundred minimum." He held the money out. Polokov's arrogance had disappeared, but Krakin didn't like the begging that had replaced it any better.

Krakin hesitated. He glanced at the two students. From their expressions they obviously thought Polokov was being a fool. Krakin took the money.

Polokov smiled. "Thank you, Krakin." He sounded genuinely appreciative.

Krakin put the money in his pocket. "I'm just taking this conditionally," he said loudly. "If I find out that you're asking me to do anything against the interest of the State, it will be returned immediately and I'll have nothing further to do with this matter." One couldn't be too careful in entering into what might appear to be a treasonable undertaking with persons one didn't actually know. Polokov looked sort of surprised and puzzled by Krakin's words, but he didn't say anything.

"What other information can I give you, Krakin?" Polokov asked.

"I believe I've got enough to start on, unless there's something else you think I ought to know."

"Not that I can recall at the moment."

"There are several things I want to pursue on my own. Then I'll get back to you." Krakin turned toward the two students. "I'd like to know if either of you has ever mentioned the manuscript to anyone."

"Never," said Kirus, shaking his head vigorously. The girl echoed his answer.

"Have you discussed the experiments with anyone?"

"Not the results. Not anything that would indicate we disagreed with the Academy. Professor Polokov made the importance of secrecy very clear to us. We're involved in this, too, you know." This time the girl spoke and Kirus nodded.

Krakin stood up. "All right. Today is Monday. I'll be in touch with you again by Wednesday. Will you be here?"

"I'm here in my office at this time every morning, and late in the afternoon. Other times I'm teaching in the biology laboratory. You will start on this right away, won't you, Krakin?"

"Yes, I will. In the mean time, you keep looking for your manuscript yourself. It still may turn out that you misplaced it. And if you find it, let me know as soon as possible, will you?"

"Yes. Of course."

Krakin nodded and let himself out of the tiny office. He had had enough of those three for the time being. He wanted to find out, through his own channels, whether there was anything to this. It was plain that Polokov and his assistants weren't going to give him any more useful information. Not intentionally, anyway. Krakin didn't think he was going to like this assignment. He patted his pocket with the money in it. That consoled him a little.

4

Krakin caught Anya just as she was about to go to lunch. She worked on the staff of the University Administrator and, like the other staff members, had a desk in the large, cathedral-like hall near the Administrator's office. Though she was the youngest, and thereby the lowest-ranking, member of the staff, she had the same perquisites as the other staff members, including access to the University files.

Anya and Krakin walked together down the wide concrete steps to the cafeteria in the basement of the Administration Building. As they went, Krakin explained briefly what Polokov wanted him to do. Anya still wore her coat, as she often did inside the building on these cold winter days. They both hung their coats up in the basement hall and went into the cafeteria.

Most students who ate here hadn't yet arrived, but the enormous room was still noisy. The smell of cooking soup and cabbage, and the warmth given off by the stoves, made the cafeteria a pleasant place to be on a day like this. Krakin and Anya each took a bowl of thick soup, black bread and tea. Some of the booths around the walls of the room were still unoccupied, and they sat down in one directly under the huge portrait of Premier Khrushchev, whose plump face gazed unblinkingly down at them from beside an even larger portrait of Lenin.

"I don't feel very comfortable talking to you while he's up there," Anya said, pointing to the picture.

"Would you like me to take him down?"

"If you can do it without being arrested."

"Then I'm afraid he stays. Look, he's got more important things to think about than us. What have you found out?"

Anya took a spoonful of soup. "Not very much yet. Polokov is Chairman of the Biology Department. He's been here almost twenty years. He's no genius, but he's as qualified as anybody else in this place."

"Any family?"

"He's married. Wife's name is Maria. No children."

"Very interesting, He didn't mention that. Anything else?"

Anya took a bite of bread and shook her head. "I haven't had a chance to check any further."

"What about the two students? Kirus and Togorny."

"They're better than average students. Kirus is actually doing Kandidatura. He had the credits to complete his university program at the end of the year. The girl will finish her university credits this summer. Do you think they took the manuscript?"

"I don't know. I don't like them, but so far I haven't discovered any reason for them to have done it."

"Maybe they realized the book was damaging to them."

"Maybe, but they should have realized that before they got this far. Does it make sense that they would work on the project for years, then steal the manuscript to avoid being involved?"

"Not if you say it doesn't."

Krakin reached across the table and took Anya's hand. "I'm

not rejecting your suggestion. You've proved me wrong too many times."

They both ate some more. "What do you want me to do next?" Anya asked after a few minutes.

"If you have time, there are several things I'd like you to check out. First of all, I'd like you to see if you can get anything further on Polokov and his two assistants"

Anya nodded, her mouth full of bread.

"Next, I'd like you to look at the files on the other people in Polokov's department. You know what I'm interested in. Anything that would give any of them a reason to take the manuscript."

"You trust my judgment?"

"Implicitly."

"Then I'll do what I can."

Krakin took Anya's hand again and held it. "There's one final thing that would be very helpful."

Anya sighed. "You sure take advantage of me."

"This is very important. I want you to get in touch with that friend of yours, what's her name, Karin something."

"Karin Mekorian."

"Yes. That's the girl. The one who works at the KGB."

Anya looked alarmed. She put her hand to her mouth, then leaned forward. "Don't say that out loud," she whispered. "You're not supposed to know it."

Krakin glanced upward at the portrait of Premier Khrushchev. "Sorry. I hope he's not listening. Anyway, I want you to ask Karin if she knows whether her . . . employer has had anything to do with the Polokov manuscript. If it has, there's no reason for me to continue on this."

"I hate to do that, Leo. She might get in trouble. Besides, she probably doesn't know. She's just a clerk."

"She has access to files, doesn't she?"

"Yes. Some files."

"Look, I don't want much. I just want to know if the KGB is involved in this. A simple yes or no. Surely that doesn't require her to take much of a risk. Just ask her. If she says no, okay."

Anya stared into Krakin's eyes. Then she sat back resignedly. "I'll ask her. She won't refuse. I'm a good friend, and she doesn't have many."

"Good girl. Tell her I'll take her out to dinner and the ballet."

Anya's eyes narrowed. "Like hell you will. Not unless you take me, too."

Krakin shrugged. "Now who's taking advantage? All right, I'll take you both to dinner and the ballet."

"At the same time."

"At the same time."

"You're so thoughtful, Leo. I'll get in touch with Karin right after lunch."

5

Underneath the piers supporting the modern concrete roadway that ran along Basilgrad's riverfront was located the city's last bastion of free enterprise. Even in February, when the river was frozen solid and the sun wasn't up until almost eight, the peasants arose in the middle of the night to bring their wagons of vegetables stored from the autumn harvest, their pork and goat's milk, and their colorful handicrafts, to market. At least in February the path that ran between the piers and the river wasn't filled with thick, soft mud as it would be in the spring and most of the summer, and there were no flies. The entrepreneurs could gather around their fires burning in empty oil drums or salvaged kerosene stoves to warm their hands and faces. The city dwellers, old women with kerchiefs over their heads, middle-aged men in faded business suits under their wool coats, even young people in their tight Western-style clothing, came to the market in the winter as they did in summer, to buy the goods that were virtually impossible to find in the government stores.

By noon the wagons were gone, to be replenished for the next day, and their owners were at work on their other jobs. At two in the afternoon, when Krakin arrived, the area was deserted. One would never have suspected the activity that had taken place there eight hours earlier, or that would occur again the next morning.

Krakin didn't stay long under the piers. Having satisfied himself that all activity had ceased for the day, he climbed back up the cracked and pitted concrete steps that led down from the roadway. He emerged from the steps onto the broad sidewalk that lay between the roadway and the buildings which fronted it. Instead of waiting to reboard a tram such as had brought him here a few minutes earlier, however, Krakin walked along the sidewalk, his eyes on the adjoining buildings.

Before the new roadway was built, some ten years earlier, these old houses, survivors from pre-Revolutionary days, had been considered desirable for their views of the river. Then, the road traffic had moved at river level, down where the market now stood, and its sights and sounds were fairly well hidden from the houses high above. Some of the buildings were so desirable as to be occupied by minor Party functionaries and important bureaucrats.

Since the roadway was constructed, however, the noise of the traffic had driven out the high-class occupants. Most of the old houses had been divided into ever smaller rooms and apartments. Now they were occupied primarily by old pensioners: couples, widows, and widowers. Younger people shunned the buildings because they represented a disappeared past; old people were attracted to them for the same reason.

Krakin found the building he was looking for. It was an old stone structure, in somewhat worse repair than its neighbors. He walked in the unlocked front door and climbed through heavy cooking odors to the third and topmost floor. On this floor, as on the others, half a dozen doors, each with a separate nameplate, faced onto a central hallway. Only on this floor, Krakin knew, the doors did not lead to separate little apartments.

Krakin opened the nearest door and went inside. He found himself in a dimly-lit cubicle measuring about three meters square. As Krakin's eyes became accustomed to the meager light he noticed an old woman in a cotton housedress sitting at a table along the side of the room. She was examining Krakin. Her face gave no sign of recognition. Finally she spoke.

"What do you mean, barging in on an old lady like this? Don't you youngsters have any manners? Get out of here."

"I'm here to see Solin," Krakin said. "I've got a very big deal to talk to him about. My name is Krakin, Mrs. Olkof. Don't you remember me?"

The old woman glared at Krakin for a moment. Then she picked up the telephone on her table and pushed a button. She waited, then spoke into it. "There's a man here named Krakin. He claims to know you and wants to talk to you." She listened. Her eyes moved up to Krakin's face. "Yes," she said. Another wait. "Yes." Then she hung up. "He'll be here to see you in a few minutes. Sit down." Krakin picked out the least dusty, least broken-down chair. It creaked when he sat on it, but it held. Krakin watched the old woman. She turned her eyes back to a magazine on the table in front of her. Krakin wondered how she could manage to read it in that poor light. Then he realized she probably couldn't; she was just looking at the pictures. In which case it wasn't the *Party Organ*. Not too many pictures in that.

The door to the hall opened and a thin, long-nosed, ascetic-looking man of about Krakin's age came into the room. Krakin stood.

"Peter Solin," Krakin said. "It's good to see you again."

Solin stepped back, his hands on his hips, taking Krakin in. "My dear Comrade Krakin, looking as young as ever. It's been a long time."

"Not that long."

Solin laughed. "That makes it sound as though you're here for business, not pleasure."

"That's right. Can we talk?"

"Sure. Come into my office. I believe I've had it redone since you were here last." He closed the door to the hall. "No need to use the formal route when it's just friends." Solin pressed the wall opposite from where the old woman sat. A hidden doorway opened, and Solin and Krakin walked through it into a very narrow, dark hallway. Solin closed the door behind them, then opened another door. Krakin followed the man into a spacious bright office, full of life and color. Impressionist and modern paintings hung on the wall; fine Turkoman carpets covered the floor. The furniture was Scandinavian. Krakin didn't care for the room, but he appreciated the costliness of the decor.

"Well, how do you like it, Krakin?" Solin asked, sitting down behind his teakwood desk.

"Very sumptuous." Krakin sat down in a metal-and-leather chair across from the desk. "You didn't buy these things at the G.U.M. And you didn't pay for them with the fees you collect from the peasants to 'protect' their market."

Solin laughed. "Correct on both counts, my dear Krakin. But then, you know what my business is. Protection is a smaller part of it all the time. I sell people what the government stores don't offer them, that's what I do. I can get just about anything you want, for a price. Just about anything. And that, I presume, is why you're here."

Krakin was tempted to try to squeeze the information he wanted out of the skinny little bastard. He would have enjoyed seeing Solin squirm. But Krakin well knew that Solin never met with anyone alone and unprotected. There were undoubtedly at least two of his bodyguards stationed just outside the office, ready to appear at a moment's notice.

"That's why I'm here," Krakin said. "But what I'm looking for is very particular. It's one of a kind."

"We handle many unique items. You are, of course, willing to pay?"

Krakin reached into his pocket and pulled out one of the three bills Polokov had given him that morning. He laid it on Solin's desk. "A token but not a measure of my client's interest."

Solin picked up the bill, held it to the light, then put it in his own pocket. "What is it you want to buy?"

"A manuscript. A recent one. By a noted scientist. It happens to contain some interesting comments on the work of the President of the Lenin Academy of Agricultural Science."

"That's not a very specific description."

"It's enough, if you have it. It's also enough for you to make inquiries about."

Solin jotted down some notes on a card in front of him. Krakin had already obtained part of the information he came for. Solin didn't know about the Polokov manuscript, and that was significant. If a professional from Basilgrad had been hired by anyone to steal the book, Solin would have known.

"Tell me, Krakin, why don't you deal directly with the author of the manuscript? Avoid the middleman."

"I have reason to believe the manuscript has already come into the possession of middlemen."

Solin frowned. "Well, we'll soon find out. Are you sure you don't want to tell me any more about it? It might speed things up."

"You have enough to go on. I want to let you earn your fee."

"Very well. Now, what sort of a fee are we talking about?"

Krakin shrugged. "I'll recommend any fair price to my client. Why don't you see how hard it is to find before we talk money? I'm sure you wouldn't take advantage of me."

Solin laughed. "Of course not." Solin put the tips of his fingers together and stared at Krakin. "Who is your client?"

"I'm afraid I can't tell you."

Solin appeared a bit piqued. "It may make a difference as to the price. If you won't tell me, I'll have to assume your client is a person of means."

"Assume what you like."

"Ah, Krakin, you don't do a very good job of concealment," Solin said triumphantly. "I ask myself, who would want a manuscript such as you describe? Who would be willing to pay a large sum for it? And what sort of person who would want it and be willing to pay for it would be likely to come into contact with a journalist such as yourself? The answer is obvious. It's one of the Western publishers touring the country at this very minute. I happen to know they'll be in

Basilgrad later this week, after they finish their visit in Leningrad. You see, it's part of my business to know about foreign nationals in our country. You really didn't think you'd be able to keep your client from me, did you? But I'm an honorable man, Krakin. Others might be tempted to go directly to the customer. I will continue to deal through you."

Krakin shook his head slowly. "You're amazing, Peter, just amazing. And a man of honor."

"Thank you, Krakin." Solin pointed a finger at Krakin. "Now let me give you a word of advice. This is risky business, working for foreigners. Smuggling books out of the country. Not what you're used to, Krakin. This you'll be punished for, if you're caught. You really ought to leave this sort of thing entirely to professionals like myself."

Krakin smiled. "You're not talking me out of this one, Peter. Just find me that manuscript."

Solin smiled back. "Very well. But I'm serious about the danger. Be careful, Krakin. I like you. I really do." He stood up from his desk in a way that said the discussion was finished. "Enough of business. Won't you have a drink with me before you go? We can have a pleasant conversation about more interesting things."

Krakin got out of his chair. "I'm afraid not this time, Peter. I've a great deal to do. Perhaps next time."

"Perhaps," Solin said dreamily. He put his hand on Krakin's arm and led him toward the door. Krakin stiffened at the contact but said nothing. Solin opened the door and Krakin stepped out into the hallway.

"You know where to reach me if you find anything," Krakin said. "If I don't hear from you, I'll stop back in a few days."

"Very good. Please be sure to bring money when you do. Thank you, Krakin. Always a pleasure to do business with you."

"Good bye, Peter." Krakin walked to the stairs. He heard the door close behind him. He smiled as he descended to the street level. He had learned more from Solin than he had hoped. Soon he would have to confront Polokov with the information.

6

Krakin was busy in the small kitchen of his apartment. Normally a single man didn't merit complete cooking facilities, not when several thousand families were on waiting lists for them. But a few favors, and a few rubles, and an apartment manager could accidentally fail to report a vacancy, and consequently the department that kept the waiting list wouldn't try to fill it, and it was available to the highest bidder. Krakin's outside income had thus far made him the highest bidder for this one. He couldn't have done it on his salary alone.

The successful visit with Solin called for a celebration, so Krakin had braved the long queue at the butcher's on the way home. He had purchased some sausages and potatoes, which he was now peeling and plopping into a pot of boiling water on the stove. The steam from the pot had already fogged over the kitchen windows. He had bought enough for two. Anya would be stopping by on her way home from work, and Krakin was sure he could persuade her to stay.

The door to the apartment opened in the other room. "Leo," Anya called. She sounded upset. Krakin put the knife down, wiped his hands on a towel, and went to see her.

"Hi. I was just fixing us something to eat."

"Oh, Leo, I'm frightened." Anya, her coat still on, rushed into Krakin's arms. Krakin hugged her and patted her gently. He tried not to show his worry. Anya didn't often get upset over trivialities.

After a moment Krakin, still holding Anya's arms, stepped back from her. "Now, what's this all about?" He guided her over to the sofa, where they both sat.

"Leo, it's Karin. She's gone, and I'm afraid they're going to come after us."

"What happened?"

"Well, you asked me at lunch to ask Karin to check the KGB files on Polokov. So I went over to see her right afterward. It isn't the sort of thing you ask a KGB employee to do on the telephone, you know, and the KGB office isn't that far away. Well, I managed to catch her on her way back from lunch, and I told her what we needed, and she agreed to see if she could find out anything for us. Well, along toward the end of the afternoon I realized I hadn't made any arrangement to see Karin later. I didn't think it would hurt to call her about that, so I did. She wasn't there." Anya looked deep into Krakin's eyes. "They told me she'd been sent to another office. Someplace way to the east. Sverdlovsk, I think they said."

Krakin held Anya's hands tightly. He felt a sudden chill. Why Sverdlovsk? ''Maybe it was some kind of mistake."

Anya shook her head. Her blond hair waved back and forth in front of her face. "I don't think so. I called back half an hour later and was told the same thing. On my way here after work I stopped by Karin's apartment. She wasn't there. I asked the manager if she knew where Karin was, and she told me she had received a call earlier today informing her that Karin would be away for a while. She wouldn't tell me any more. She might have known that the KGB was involved."

"This is terrible. Poor Karin. I'm so sorry."

"Oh, Leo, I know. But what about us?" Anya returned to Krakin's arms and he held her close to him. He felt the fear that still, despite the reforms that had taken place in the nearly ten years since Stalin's death, lay so near the thoughts of every Soviet citizen. The fear of the knock on the door in the middle of the night, the separation--perhaps forever--from one's home and loved ones. It was the separation that Krakin dreaded the most. He could survive anywhere, even in a labor camp. He knew he had what it took. He had a feel for the way the system worked. But without Anya, what would be the point? He didn't want to survive without her.

Reason returned. "What makes you think *we're* in danger?"

"Because I asked Karin to spy on the KGB for us. Don't you see? She must have got caught. That's why she's being sent away. Oh, Leo, why did you ask me to do it?"

"I'm sorry, Anya. I feel awful. But look, we don't know that's why Karin's been sent to another office. Even if it is, it doesn't mean anything's going to happen to us. Karin may not give them our names, and if she does, we haven't done anything so bad. I just wanted to find out if the KGB took Polokov's manuscript. If they did, then I was going to drop the matter. Besides, I've got some information now that leads me to believe the KGB may not have anything to do with this Polokov thing."

"Oh, Leo, I wish I felt as sure as you. But I asked Karin to look at KGB files for me. I'm sure that's a criminal offense all by itself."

"Darling, they've no reason to do anything to us. It was all perfectly innocent. But if there is trouble, I'm responsible. I won't let anything happen to you."

Anya moved closer. "If anything happens to you, it might as well happen to me."

"Well, it's already after six o'clock and they haven't come for us yet. If they want us, they won't be long."

"Leo, I want to stay here, Until we know."

"Sure. I've already got a meal on for the two of us. As a matter of fact, I haven't quite finished getting it started. Come on and help me." He took Anya's hand and pulled her into the kitchen with him. The first thing he did was reach into a cabinet and bring down a bottle of vodka and two tumblers, which he filled. They touched the glasses and drank.

"That'll make you feel better," Krakin said.

"I wish I had your courage."

Krakin smiled. The weakness in his knees hadn't yet betrayed him. He took another sip of vodka.

Anya sat down at the little oilcloth covered table. "You said you had some information that the KGB may not be involved with Polokov. What did you find?"

Krakin picked up his knife and began peeling another potato. "I went to see my old friend Peter Solin this afternoon."

"Ugh."

"Yes, I know. But Peter is a useful person. If anyone was hired to steal Polokov's manuscript, Peter would be likely to know of it. In any event, he gave me the motive for the theft. Our friend Polokov held something back."

"What's that?" Krakin could tell that the vodka was calming Anya. He felt a little bit better himself.

"A group of Western publishers is touring the country. They're in Leningrad now. They're scheduled to be in Basilgrad this week. Solin thinks one or more of them would be interested in buying the manuscript. As a matter of fact, Solin thinks I'm working for one of them." Krakin laughed.

"I don't understand. Why would a Western publisher want to buy a book by a third-rate Soviet biology professor?"

"They want to buy it because they can sell it. Don't you see, it doesn't make any difference what the author's credentials are. It probably doesn't even make much difference what he says. It's the fact that a Soviet citizen has dared to stand up to the Academy of Science. He'll be a hero in the West, and books by heros sell very well."

"Why does Solin think you're working for the Westerners?" Anya asked, taking a long drink from her glass and setting it gently back on the table.

Krakin tilted his head. "His own incorrect deduction. Solin wouldn't make a very good investigator. Of course, I didn't disagree with his conclusion. If he thinks I've got money behind me, he'll work harder to find the manuscript."

"Solin could be wrong about the Western publishers wanting the book, too. After all, Polokov didn't say anything about it."

"That's true." Krakin tried very hard to treat Anya's comment reasonably. "But it does all fit together. Why would Polokov hire me to find the missing book otherwise? He wouldn't want to spend the money. His story about Lysenko and the Academy of Science never really did ring true. I grant you that the Academy, and consequently the KGB, may have reason to be interested in the manuscript." Krakin wished he hadn't said that; he continued hastily. "But Polokov should know that there's nothing I can do to help him if the Academy or the KGB is involved. Therefore there's got to be another reason for

Polokov retaining me."

"Maybe Polokov just wants to prevent the book from falling into the hands of the KGB."

Krakin thought. "That's possible, I grant you. But it doesn't seem nearly as likely as the possibility that someone stole the manuscript in order to sell it."

"And that," Anya said triumphantly, "makes Polokov's two students the prime suspects."

Krakin was taken aback for a moment. "You know, I believe you're right," he said. "Tell me, did you find out anything more about them?" Krakin noted that Anya's glass was empty. He refilled it and topped off his own.

Anya shook her head. "There were other people in the file room all afternoon. I was afraid they would ask me what I was doing. I'll try to get the material on them tomorrow. And also the other information you asked for."

"Good girl. Here's to you." Krakin lifted his glass and took a deep drink. He was starting to feel just the slightest bit silly.

"If I can still go to work tomorrow." The brightness evaporated from Anya's face, and Krakin sobered rapidly. "Here we are talking as if nothing was wrong--as if Karin was still around." She looked as if she was about to cry. Krakin moved to her side and put his arm around her shoulder. She looked up at him.

"Oh, Leo, what do we say if they come? What do we tell them?"

"We tell them exactly what happened. The whole truth. Anya, we couldn't make up anything that was more innocent. We haven't done anything that would concern the KGB."

"I hope you're right. It makes me feel better to hear you say it."

"I am right. Now, why don't you help me with this dinner. There's a lot to do." Krakin wished that what he had said was as much comfort to him as it appeared to be to Anya.

7

Krakin stirred in the bed he shared with Anya, and as he did, she, still asleep, snuggled closer to him. He smiled drowsily. Suddenly he opened his eyes. His slowly returning consciousness had brought with it the memory of the previous evening.

Now he saw the daylight beginning to filter into the room. It was morning. He and Anya were still in his apartment. Alone. Everything was just as it had been the night before.

He slipped out of bed and put on his robe. He went into the kitchen, heated some water and made tea. Then he filled the bowl in the bathroom with hot water and shaved slowly. When he returned to the living room Anya was just raising herself to a sitting position in the bed.

"We're still here," Krakin said. He went to the window and raised one of the shades. It was a clear day. Krakin could feel the bitter cold coming in through the glass.

"Do you think we're safe?" Anya asked, still not fully awake.

"It looks pretty good."

Anya appeared more alert. "Maybe they tried to pick me up at my apartment."

"The manager would have sent them over here first thing."

"Then maybe they're not going to come after us."

"It looks that way."

Anya waited a minute, rubbing her eyes. Krakin sat down next to her. "Leo," Anya said tentatively, "this isn't one of your tricks, is it?"

"What do you mean?"

"Making me think last night might be our last night together."

"Anya! Would I do anything so cruel?"

Anya looked into Krakin's eyes. "No, I guess not. So clever, yes. But not so cruel." She paused. Krakin put his arm around her. "Leo," she said, "would you do a favor for me?"

"Sure. Anything."

"Would you take me to work this morning? Just to make sure they're not waiting for me there."

"Of course. I need to go to the University again, anyway. To see Polokov."

"Thank you, Leo." She leaned over to kiss him. They embraced and clung together for a long time.

8

Krakin dropped Anya off at her office shortly after nine. They purposely went late, so that any KGB agent would already be there when they arrived. None was. Everything was perfectly normal. Anya seemed greatly relieved. Krakin left her and went over to the Biological Sciences Building.

The building had entrances on each of its four sides. Krakin went into the one nearest Polokov's office. A stairway just inside led to the empty second floor corridor. The second door down the hall was Polokov's. It would, Krakin concluded, be relatively easy for someone to slip into the building and go to Polokov's office undetected, especially if such a person was familiar with the schedules of the professor and his students.

Krakin knocked on Polokov's door. There was no answer. He tried it, and it opened easily. As Polokov had said, there was no lock.

Krakin turned on the lights. The place was the same as it had been yesterday, messy and disorganized. He went to the shelf where Polokov said the manuscript had been kept and rubbed his finger along it. Dusty, but not very dusty. There was space behind the adjacent books. Curious, Krakin felt behind them. Nothing.

"Well, Krakin, have you found it so soon?" Polokov's voice crackled from the doorway.

Krakin turned to face the man. He wore the same clothes as yesterday. Krakin wondered if he had even removed them overnight.

"I'm afraid not. I came back to ask you a few more questions."

"Don't tell me you haven't started yet!"

Krakin laughed without humor. "Oh, I've started. I've already managed to spend a good part of what you gave me. And I've got a friend in trouble with the KGB."

"What do you mean by that?"

"I asked a friend who is a clerk at the KGB offices to find out if the KGB is involved in this matter. A few hours later my friend was sent to Sverdlovsk."

Polokov turned pale. He stepped unsteadily to his desk and sat down behind it. "Does he know about me?"

"Of course. I couldn't very well ask about your manuscript without giving out your name."

"You fool! Now the KGB will be after all of us. How could you be so stupid? What am I going to do?"

Krakin walked up next to Polokov and looked down at him. "Polokov, if you'd given me all the information at the beginning we wouldn't be in this mess."

"What do you mean?"

"I mean, if you'd told me you planned to sell the book to a Western publisher this week, I wouldn't have been paying so much attention to the KGB. I would have been looking for someone with a profit motive."

Polokov swallowed. He looked toward the door, which was still slightly open. He got up and closed it, then looked back at Krakin.

"How do you know about selling the book?"

"That's my business. Did you really think I wouldn't find out?"

Polokov returned to his desk. "Look, Krakin," he said apologetically, "I wasn't trying to keep anything from you. I just didn't want them to know."

"Them?"

"Kirus and Togorny. My students. If they knew the book was to be published, they might try to stop it. Their reputations, you know."

"Or maybe they might want a share of the money?"

Polokov looked into Krakin's face but didn't say anything.

"How much are you going to get?"

"That's none of your business."

Krakin shrugged and started for the door. "I can't help you if you don't tell me everything."

"Wait! All right. They're going to pay me 15,000 rubles. Or were, before you messed everything up. What are we going to do about the KGB, Krakin?" Polokov's voice was desperate.

"My friend was sent away yesterday afternoon. Assuming that looking into the files was what caused the transfer--and we don't know that for sure--the KGB would have known about us yesterday. If they were going to do anything to us, they would've done it by now."

"But they still know about us. They know what I'm trying to do."

"Not necessarily. All they will find out is that I asked a friend to look at your file, which I happen to know they have. If they check further, they'll find out that I told my editor yesterday morning I was thinking of writing an article about you. So there's nothing to be suspicious about."

"Is that what you'll tell them if they ask you-- that you're writing an article about me?"

"No. The KGB is pretty good at determining whether they've been told the truth. I'll tell them that you hired me to find your manuscript."

Polokov wrung his hands. "What am I to do, Krakin? Should I go ahead?"

"That's up to you. I don't want to have anything to do with selling the book, if that's your purpose. But if you still want me to find the book, I'm willing to do that—for my fee, of course."

"Damn!" Polokov struck the desk with his bony fist. He looked down and started tugging at his cheeks, so hard that red marks appeared on his pale skin. He looked up again at Krakin. "Find it for me, Krakin."

"All right. You'll have to answer a few more questions, then."

"Go ahead."

"How do you know you can sell your book for 15,000?"

"A man came to see me. I'd never seen him before. He said he wasn't from around here. He asked if I had written up my research, and I told him about the book. He said a Western publisher would be willing to buy it for 15,000 if it was finished by this week. I said I'd sell it. I worked like crazy to get it finished in time. Then all this happened. All that work for nothing, unless you find it."

"What was this man's name? Did he say?"

"Tvori. Laszlo Tvori. He said he came from Leningrad. The publisher sent him. I have the publisher's name too." Polokov rummaged through a messy drawer of his desk. "Putney. Horace Putney. An American."

"Did this Tvori say how the publisher knew about you?"

"No."

"Didn't you think it odd that an American was interested in your book when you haven't even told your own colleagues about it?"

"I suppose so. But when he mentioned the money, and the number of people who would probably read my book, I forgot about that."

"Are you sure you've told me about everyone who knows of the manuscript?"

"Yes. Now I have. I'm not holding anything else back."

"What about your wife?"

"My wife?"

"Doesn't she know about your book? You didn't tell me about her."

"Yes, she knows. But she's my wife."

"Does she want you to sell the book? Does she want it published?"

Polokov made nervous, swinging movements with his hands. "No. She's afraid. But I'm sure she didn't have anything to do with this."

"I don't care what you think," said Krakin, letting a note of irritation creep into his voice. "I want to know everything, whether you think it's important or not."

Polokov cowered. "I'm sorry, Krakin." He pulled at his lips with his fingers, thinking. "I'm sure I've told you about everyone now."

"All right. When did this Tvori come here?"

"Early last week. On Monday, a week ago yesterday. He came late in the afternoon, just as I was about to leave my office."

"Did anyone else see him?"

"Not that I know of. I was alone in my office. The students have usually left the building by then."

"What did he say, other than what you've told me already?"

Polokov thought for a moment. "I've told you everything. He was only here for a few minutes."

"Well, did he look at the manuscript?" Krakin demanded, irritated again.

"Oh, yes. I showed it to him."

"Did he see where you kept it?"

"Well, naturally. I took it down to show it to him."

"And you told him it wasn't finished. Did he seem surprised?"

Polokov spread his palms. "How am I to know that?"

"All right. When are you supposed to deliver the manuscript?"

"Saturday. When the publishers come to Basilgrad. Putney is going to get in touch with me. They leave from here Sunday to go back to the West. What am I going to tell him, Krakin?"

Krakin didn't bother to answer Polokov's plea. It was obvious what he had to do now. Polokov wasn't going to give him any more information he couldn't deduce for himself. "Well, that covers it for now, Professor," he said abruptly. "Would you please give me another two hundred rubles?"

"What for?"

"Expenses. I'm going to Leningrad to see Mr. Putney." Polokov looked at Krakin in amazement. "You mean you can leave the city, just like that?" He attempted to snap his fingers. "What about your employer? Your papers?"

"I've got the papers to go just about anyplace in the country. My Chief Editor assumes I'm working for him. We journalists have a few privileges. Now, the money, please."

Polokov continued to stare at Krakin, Finally, without a word he reached into his jacket pocket, withdrew his wallet, removed two bills and handed them to Krakin. Surprised at the lack of resistance, Krakin wished he had said three hundred.

9

Krakin stopped briefly to see Anya again and tell her his plans. She wasn't overjoyed about his leaving town, but nothing further had happened to suggest that the KGB was interested in them, and Anya seemed much more at ease about that. She still hadn't finished checking the files on Polokov's students. Krakin left her and waited what seemed like half an hour on the icy, windy corner at the edge of the University grounds for the tram that eventually appeared to take him to the Square.

He hadn't been at his desk at the *Party Organ* office for more than five minutes when Ivan Sulka came up to him.

"I see you're finally here, Krakin."

"Yes. I was working on an article."

"I'd like to talk with you. Please come back to my office."

Krakin rose and followed Sulka back behind his partition. "There's something I need to ask you for, too, Ivan," Krakin said as they crossed in front of the desks of the other workers.

Sulka sat behind his desk. Krakin remained standing. "Now, Krakin," Sulka said, "about that article you told me you were planning yesterday--the one about the professor."

"Polokov?" Krakin felt suddenly uneasy.

"Yes. That's the one. Krakin, I've been thinking about that, and I just don't believe it's a very good subject. I suggest you drop it and go on to something more suitable for our magazine."

Krakin felt like the bottom dropped out of his belly. He forced himself to relax. Sulka usually took no interest in Krakin's articles until they were finished. Someone had been around asking questions.

"Sure thing, Ivan," Krakin said with as much cheerfulness as he could muster. "This Polokov isn't turning out to be what I expected anyway. As a matter of fact, that's why I wanted talk to you. I've got an idea for a new article, and I need your help to get to work on it."

"I'm listening." Sulka seemed pleased, undoubtedly relieved that Krakin had given up so easily on Polokov. Sulka hated complications, especially when they appeared to involve the KGB.

"I've heard that a group of western publishers is touring the country. They'll be coming here Saturday, but only for a short time. Until then they'll be in Leningrad. I think there may be a good article there. A real, serious ideological article. You know, showing how their system of using profit to determine which books are published destroys literature and distorts the truth."

Sulka beamed. "I *like* that, Krakin. A good idea. That's much better than this Polokov thing. The Central Committee will love it, if they ever read it. I'll even *suggest* they read it."

"Then you won't mind authorizing me to go to Leningrad."

Sulka frowned momentarily. "You won't have enough time with these publishers when they get to Basilgrad?"

"They'll be much too busy with other things here getting ready to leave the country."

Sulka's smile returned. "All right. Go ahead. It will probably be good for you to get out of Basilgrad for a while."

Krakin wondered for a moment what Sulka meant, then gave up on it. "I'd like to go tomorrow morning."

Sulka shrugged. "Do a nice job for me now."

10

Krakin worked at his desk the rest of the morning outlining the new article he had suggested to his editor. He struggled with each sentence and gazed out the window for a long time between them. When he completed the first section, he allowed himself to walk to the back of the room to get a drink of water. After he completed the second, he went to the men's room. After the third, the water fountain again.

Krakin gazed at the empty space on the paper where the fourth section would go. How did he ever get into an occupation so unsuited to his natural inclinations, he wondered. He should be in the same business as Peter Solin. No, he was too considerate of people he liked. Party work, then. Organizing and endlessly currying favor. He wouldn't mind that too much, but he couldn't stand the endless meetings and lectures on socialist theory.

What he liked to do best, Krakin thought, was to solve problems like that of Professor Polokov. Not because he cared about Polokov, but because he liked solving the puzzle. He liked getting information he wasn't supposed to have, devising ruses to do things a citizen wasn't ordinarily allowed to do. He should have been born in the West. In America. Why, according to their books (not the Mark Twain or the Sinclair Lewis in the Party-approved translations, but the uncensored modern books of the sort Peter Solin sold), there were men in the United States who made their entire living as private investigators. Hundreds of them, to judge by the number of books about them. Krakin contemplated blissfully the thought of being free to pursue such an occupation full time.

But the outline wasn't getting written. Perhaps he could call one of the people in his writers' group and get him to write the article. It was, after all, a very good idea and sure to be well received.

Unfortunately, however, one of the rules of the writers' group which Krakin himself insisted be strictly enforced was no communications except at the meetings on Sunday evenings. Too many bosses, including Krakin's own, would not approve their workers pursuing such additional employment.

Krakin composed another section. As he constructed the outline on one pad of paper, he also kept a second pad next to it to jot down thoughts that occurred to him out of the logical order but which he didn't want to lose. Polokov's problem kept getting mixed in his mind with the article. He pulled the second pad over and wrote: "What is the effect of profit orientation on development of the most gifted writers? Do they adapt to the system? Or do they fail to survive? Perhaps explore at the end of the article." Krakin read over the note. The same question might be asked, he supposed, as to the effect of socialist orientation on gifted writers. But, of course, he would never dare write that question down, not even in his own private notes.

By one o'clock, when it was time for lunch, Krakin had got more than halfway through the outline. He could, he rationalized, finish it later. After a quick bite to eat, he hopped on a tram going to the riverfront.

11

Solin was sitting in one of the modern lounge chairs in his office, a scowl on his face. He didn't look up until a minute or two after the old woman let Krakin in. Solin was reading, Krakin noted with surprise, a copy of the *Party Organ*.

"Back so soon, Krakin?" Solin finally said, putting down the magazine. "You said several days."

"I have to go to Leningrad to work on an article. I don't know when I'll be back, so I thought I'd check with you before I leave."

"To Leningrad? To write an article? Come now, Krakin. Is this article for Eastern or Western consumption?"

"Its for the *Party Organ.*" Krakin pointed at the magazine Solin had put down. "You can read it sometime next month."

"All right. Have it your way. But say hello to your publisher friends while you're there, okay?"

Krakin smiled. "I'd like to be able to say you've found the manuscript, but I doubt that you have."

"Why do you say that?"

"Because the people who I have reason to suspect took it are not people you would know about."

"Then you would be surprised if I told you I have the manuscript already?"

Krakin was surprised. "Do you have it?"

"Do you have the money? I asked you to bring it next time."

"How much do you want?"

Solin pursed his lips thoughtfully and tapped his fingers on the chrome arm of his chair. "Twenty thousand."

"No deal. It's not worth that to anyone. Five thousand is all my client can pay. I'll have to threaten him a little to get him to approve that."

Solin shook his head. "You forget, Krakin, that I have to pay for the book. Fifteen thousand is the lowest I can go and still show any profit myself."

"And you forget that my client has to pay me over and above what he pays you. Five thousand or no deal."

"What the hell, I'll give up my profit. Twelve thousand five hundred."

Krakin smiled. "Peter, you're not going to sell the manuscript unless I buy it. You'll be stuck. And besides, if you paid more than twenty five hundred for it, you're a fool. I don't think you're a fool. Five thousand, and that's it."

Solin sighed. "You're a hard bargainer, Krakin. It's a buyer's market. Very well, five thousand. I'll take a loss, but I seem to have no choice. Anyway, it's for an old friend. Now, where is the money?"

"Where is the book?"

"It's on its way here."

"So is the money."

Solin looked at Krakin quizzically. Krakin smiled again, then broke into a hearty laugh. "You son of a bitch," Krakin said, "you don't have the book!"

Solin laughed too, a high-pitched, feminine laugh, almost a giggle. "And you don't have any money."

"Then what the hell are we doing?"

"You have given me some information. I know how much I can spend to get the manuscript. We have established a floor for the negotiations when I do."

"What do you mean, a floor? We have a deal. Five thousand if you find the book."

"Ah, but you don't have the money, so there is no contract. Besides, you didn't think I would bargain as easily as that if it were for real, did you?"

"Well, at least I have some information myself. The book wasn't taken by any of the local professionals, or you would know by now. I'm afraid, Peter, that this one isn't in your line."

Solin shrugged. "We'll see, Krakin. We'll see." He got up from his chair. "Will you have a drink with me today, Krakin?"

Krakin nodded. It would he an affront to decline Solin a second time in two days. "Vodka, please." Solin went to a rosewood cabinet and took out a bottle of vodka and a bottle of Spanish sherry for himself. He poured the drinks and handed Krakin his. Then he went over to his chair and picked up the copy of the *Party Organ* that he had put aside a few minutes earlier.

"You know, Krakin," Solin said, "I used to be able to identify your articles in here just by their quality. I can't do that any more. Are you slipping?"

Krakin drank. "Maybe."

"Or perhaps you are merely editing articles these days?"

"Something like that."

Solin smiled and put the magazine down. He and Krakin talked a few minutes longer about common friends and common enemies. As soon as Krakin could, he excused himself and left Solin to his Oriental rugs, his Scandinavian furniture, and his Russian bodyguards.

12

Krakin found himself more productive when he returned to the office. Perhaps seeing Solin had curbed his dissatisfaction with his own job. In any event, he finished the outline and had even written a few opening paragraphs by four, when he decided he could use a change of scene. He tried to call Anya, but he was told she was busy in the file room. Krakin wondered for a moment if his inability to reach Anya was cause for concern and decided it wasn't. He gathered up his train tickets, his internal passport, and his other documents and went home, where he took off his shoes and stretched out on his sofa. He must have dozed for fifteen or twenty minutes, for the next thing he knew he awoke to a much darker apartment. He started to reach for a lamp when he sensed a movement in the room near the door. He had been awakened by someone coming into the room. Another noise sounded, closer to the door. Krakin tensed, then leaped out of bed toward the noise. As he moved he saw the gray shape of a small person, slightly to the left of where he had heard the noise. He reached out to grab the intruder but succeeded only in getting a good whack on a thin, narrow shoulder. Both Krakin and the other fell to the floor. Krakin scrambled after the person but stopped short as a thin voice cried out.

"Ow! You hurt my shoulder, you ape!" Then came sobbing. It was a woman's voice, but not one Krakin recognized.

He stood up and turned on the lamp near the door. A slender woman, with dark hair and dark eyes, sat hunched over on the floor, holding her shoulder. The lamp shone brightly on her face. She had severe, but not unattractive, features. Her skin was that of a woman in her mid-thirties, but her figure, even under her long gray dress, was girlish.

"This really hurts. God, I think you might have broken it." She was holding back tears, but only with great effort.

"I'm sorry, but what do you expect when you sneak around in someone else's apartment?"

She glared at him. "I wasn't sneaking around. I had just come in when you jumped on me."

"What do you want?"

"Are you Leo Krakin?"

"Yes."

The woman's expression softened. "I came to see you. I must talk with you."

"You could've just knocked on the door. I would've let you in."

"I did. Nothing happened. So I tried the door. It opened. I didn't think anyone was home, so I came in to wait for you."

Krakin considered whether to believe the woman's story or not. Perhaps it didn't make any difference. He reached out a hand to the woman. "Here, let me help you up. There's a place to sit that's more comfortable than the floor."

The woman took Krakin's hand and let him pull her to her feet, She felt surprisingly light. Krakin sat her down on the sofa. She continued to hold her shoulder.

"Would you like me to look at your shoulder?"

"No. You're no doctor."

Krakin looked into the woman's dark eyes. "How do you know about me? Who are you?"

"I'm Maria Polokov. I came to see you about the job you are doing for my husband."

"You're married to Professor Polokov?" Krakin asked incredulously.

"Yes."

"You're not old enough."

The woman smiled faintly. "He's much older than I. We met at the University when I was a student. My passion was ballet, not biology, in case you wondered. He comforted me when I failed in the tryouts for the State Ballet. He asked me to marry him and I said yes. At the time it seemed the only way to salvage something of my life." She spoke neither defensively nor bitterly.

"And now?"

"Perhaps there was nothing to be salvaged."

Krakin sat down across from the woman. "Why do you want to see me?"

"I want to ask you to stop working for my husband. I don't want his manuscript found."

"But why? Are you aware of the financial considerations?"

"Yes. He's told me everything. No amount of money is enough to pay for being sent to a labor camp."

"Is that what you think will happen if the book is published?"

"I'm certain of it. Not me, perhaps, but certainly my husband."

"The professor doesn't seem to be worried about that."

"He is a single-minded, naive man. He can't see beyond the money and the fame he supposes he'll get from the book."

"Maybe to him those things are worth the labor camp."

"They're not. He may think so, but he would never survive the camps."

"It's still his decision, not yours. Go make your arguments to him, not me."

The woman glared at Krakin for a moment. "You don't care about people, do you? You just want your filthy money. I know your type. You'll do anything, as long as it gets you what you want. You have no principles. No conscience."

Krakin stood up, angry. He fought off an urge to strike the woman again. He stepped instead to the door and jerked it open. "There's nothing wrong with helping a man try to obtain the rewards he thinks he's earned, whatever they are. I'm not so wise that I can put myself in the position of deciding what's best for other people. I'm not the State. Please leave."

Maria Polokov didn't get up. After a moment she bent over and put her hands to her face. "I'm sorry," she said between sobs. "I'm just so frightened. I'm afraid of the KGB. I don't want to be involved with them." She raised her face to Krakin, her eyes wet. "Please, Mr. Krakin, I'll pay you more than my husband. I'll do *anything* for you. *Anything*. Just stop looking for that book."

Krakin sat down next to her. She turned to him and threw her arms around him, wincing with the pain in her shoulder. She pressed herself against him.

Krakin gently pushed her away but left his arm loosely around her shoulders. "Mrs. Polokov," he said, "despite what you think, I have as many principles as a man is permitted to have. I've accepted a job from your husband, whom I don't really like very much, and I'm going to continue to do it as long as he wants me to. You tell him how you feel. I'll help you; I'll make sure he knows what the risks are, if he doesn't already. If he tells me to stop, I will. But until he does, I must go on."

The woman moved back to Krakin, this time to bury her head in his shoulder. She cried a bit longer, then finally stopped and pulled back, wiping her eyes. "Please do what you can, Krakin. For me." She stood up. "I must go now." She turned and quickly left, through the still-opened door. Krakin sat looking after her for a long time after the sound of her footsteps down the wooden stairs had died out. Where, he wondered, might Maria Polokov have tried to hide her husband's book?

13

Krakin was still sitting there half an hour later when Anya came in on her way home from work.

"How nice of you to leave the door open for me," Anya said.

"I had a visitor. She left it open, and I forgot to close it."

"She?" A crease appeared in the smooth skin of Anya's forehead.

"A slim, young thing. Former ballerina. Not bad looking."

"What did she want?" Anya took a cigarette out of her purse and lit it. The act amused Krakin. Anya smoked only rarely.

"She tried to throw herself at me, but I rejected her."

"Out of loyalty and consideration for me?"

"Out of consideration for her. She was distraught."

Anya seemed to relax. She stubbed the cigarette out. "Who was she?"

"Maria Polokov. She wants me to stop looking for her husband's manuscript. She's afraid she might be taken away by the KGB."

"That's not funny." Anya's voice was sharp.

"I didn't mean it as a joke. It's what happened."

"She sounds like a sensible person. What did you tell her?"

"I told her to persuade her husband, not me. That I'll stop looking if he asks me to."

"You know, Leo, you're crazy to continue with this. You could wind up ruining a lot of lives other than your own."

"Like yours?"

"Like mine. And Karin's. And Mrs. Polokov's."

"You didn't hear from the KGB this afternoon, did you?" Krakin said, suddenly concerned.

"No. Nothing from them."

"Look, Anya, if the KGB knows about Polokov's book, and if they don't want it published, they'd have come for us by now. Therefore, we can assume either they don't know about it, or they don't care if the book is published. Either way, we're in the clear, and they can't have any serious charges against Karin. I'm sorry she's been sent away, but that could have happened anyway, for a million reasons. Anya, this whole affair puzzles me. It's a challenge. I want to solve it. We've got a new suspect, incidentally."

"Mrs. Polokov?"

"Right. She really doesn't want that book published."

"But if she took it, feeling that way, wouldn't she just destroy it? Why would she bother to come to you?"

Krakin thought for a moment, rubbing his chin. "You may be right," he said reluctantly. "She wouldn't care about preserving her husband's great research, not when she thinks her skin may be at stake."

Anya didn't say anything. She remained standing, her arms folded across her chest, looking at Krakin with a rather grim expression.

Krakin expected Anya to gloat, at least a little. When she didn't, he asked "Is something the matter? Is there something I don't know?"

Anya took a deep breath and released it. Then she moved over to the sofa and sat down next to Krakin. "I have some more information for you. I think it may tell you who has the manuscript. I also think it means we're not out of danger."

"What did you find out?"

"I finally got into the student files this afternoon and looked at the confidential folders on Kirus and Togorny. Among other things, they're both officers in the Young Communist League."

"What?"

Anya nodded vigorously. "It's true. They've both been in it since before they came to Basilgrad. For all I know, they were assigned here by the League. Togorny is secretary of the local chapter."

Krakin rubbed his chin again, considering Anya's news. "And you think that, being good Socialists and prospective Party members, they took the manuscript to keep it from being published."

"Right. Obviously they couldn't just sit by and watch it happen. They'd be held accountable if anyone later found out."

"That seems very plausible," Krakin conceded.

"And what's more, they know you're involved. If the KGB hasn't found out yet, they will eventually. Especially if you try to get the book away from those kids. You wouldn't do that, would you, Leo?"

Krakin didn't respond to the question. His mind was at work on the new facts. "What I don't understand," he said, "is what kids like that have been doing working for a heretic like Polokov for all these years."

"Remember, they were in the Komsomol even before they came to Basilgrad."

"You're not suggesting . . . . It couldn't be that . . . . But it could. That's just the sort of thing the KGB does, isn't it? They have spies everywhere."

14

Snow-covered fields and forests of birch and pine flowed endlessly past the window of Krakin's compartment as the train from Basilgrad sped northward toward the frozen canals of Leningrad. Krakin had slept late and had just made the nine o'clock departure. He planned to spend most of the ten-hour trip working on his article.

Krakin had misgivings about his journey. If Kirus and Togorny actually had taken the manuscript, then he wasn't going to learn anything helpful in Leningrad. Moreover, if the students were responsible, then the more Krakin pursued the matter, the more he was endangering himself--and Anya. He ought to have stayed in Basilgrad to check out Anya's new information. But having requested the trip, he didn't want to stir things up with Sulka by changing his mind.

Two stout old women with sun-wrinkled peasant faces shared Krakin's compartment. They chattered and cackled incessantly. One of them had apparently never been on a passenger train before, and she remarked on every smallest detail of the passing landscape. Their conversation made it difficult for Krakin to concentrate.

After considerable procrastination, Krakin began to write. He would compose the final paragraphs first. That, he had found after years of half-completed articles, was the only way to make sure he finished what he started.

"Thus it is," Krakin wrote, "that in the West the writer who survives is the writer who sells. Subsidization of gifted writers, whether by the government or by other sources, is virtually non-existent. A talent that does not adapt to modish tastes will wither and die, for it has no support other than the marketplace.

"But, Westerners will argue, is not the desire of the people the proper standard of quality for literature? Do we not in fact apply a true socialist principle in letting the coins of the masses dictate our production?

"The answer to this argument is simple. It is not truly all the people whose demand governs the production, but rather the bourgeoisie in whom the wealth of the West is concentrated. Single ethnic groups which have exploited the labor of the working classes have a greatly disproportionate power, through their purses, to dictate the literary output of their whole society.

"Furthermore, the motive of profit is a corrupting influence. The writer forgets the satisfaction of a piece of work well done in his quest for more and more money to purchase the frivolous luxuries of Western life. Contrast that situation with our own, where the talented writer is subsidized by the State at a fixed rate not dependent on the vagaries of the marketplace, and where the content of his work is governed, not by the whims of the bourgeoisie, but by the solid and lasting criteria of the peoples' cultural councils. Small wonder that the literature of our Socialist state is so immeasurably superior to that of the West."

Krakin stopped writing and re-read his paragraphs. A little stilted, perhaps, but they ought to please the Central Committee. Maybe they would put in a good word for him with the KGB. Of course, the article was based on some amount of speculation about Western literature, but it really didn't matter whether the speculation was confirmed by his interviews or not. None of his readers would ever know.

15

The train arrived in Leningrad at 7:30 p.m., only half an hour behind schedule. Krakin thought of eating at the cafe in the station but decided to wait until he arrived at the hotel. It wasn't wise to put off registering any longer than necessary. The more time passed, the more opportunity for the clerks to lose the reservation (assuming they had ever received it) and give the room to someone else. Or they might even decide to close down the desk for the evening. Krakin could always go elsewhere, but it was important that if possible he stay at the Neva where the Western publishers were.

Krakin walked the five blocks along the Nevsky Prospekt. It was cold, but not as cold as one might expect this much further north. Lake Ladoga and the Gulf of Finland seemed to exert a moderating influence on Leningrad's winter climate.

The small lobby of the Neva was warm and stuffy, but the noises of conversation and the smells of food cooking made the place inviting after five blocks through the cold. The two clerks were still on duty, but they had no record of Krakin's reservation.

"But here are my papers," Krakin pulled them out of his jacket pocket and showed them to the older clerk, a thin, bald man with wire-rimmed glasses. He looked at them perfunctorily.

"It may say you're staying here, but it doesn't say anything about a reservation."

"Well, I was told before I left Basilgrad that the reservation was made."

"We don't have any record of it."

"Well, the hell with the reservation. Do you have any rooms?"

"That is immaterial. You must have a reservation to get a room."

"Well, if you have a room, I'll make a reservation for it right now."

"Reservations must be made at least eight hours in advance. That's the rule." The clerk held up a discolored placard covered with numbered paragraphs in small type.

Krakin boiled. "Look," he began, but his proposed invective was interrupted as a man who had been sitting in a chair near the desk put down his newspaper and stepped to Krakin's side. He was not much older than Krakin, with short, close-cropped hair and clean-cut good looks. His tanned face contrasted with his even, white teeth. He was neatly dressed in a brown suit.

"Excuse me," the man said, with a slight but unmistakable American accent. "I couldn't help but overhear. I happen to know there are several unoccupied rooms near mine, No. 402, on the fourth floor. I can't imagine they're all reserved."

"But this man doesn't have a reservation," the clerk protested.

"Perhaps you could call the manager at home. I happen to know him."

The clerk turned reluctantly to the mailbox, pulled out a key, and handed it to Krakin. "Be sure to leave this with the woman on the floor when you go out," he said dully. Krakin signed for the key, then spoke to his benefactor.

"Thank you. It's odd that a foreigner has more influence here than a good Socialist citizen." He winked to the other to indicate that his words were for the clerk.

"Perhaps this fellow wants me to help him defect," the man

said, going along. The clerk paled, glanced around to see if anyone was listening, then shuffled off into an office behind the desk.

"My name is Leo Krakin. I'm from Basilgrad."

They shook hands. "Steve Andrews," the other man said. "From the United States."

"Are you here with the Western publishers?"

"Not exactly. I'm the Leningrad correspondent for a news service, but I've been helping the publishers with their arrangements while they're here. They don't speak much Russian."

"I'm a journalist myself. I write for the *Party Organ*. That's a monthly magazine published by the Party organization for the Basilgrad Region. As a matter of fact, I'm here to do an article on publishing in the West. Sort of a polemic, I'm afraid," he added, feeling slightly embarrassed.

Andrews smiled. "I have to write a few polemics myself." They both laughed. "You know," Andrews continued, "I believe I recognize your name. I'm sure I've read some of your work. If you need any help getting information from the publishers, let me know."

"Perhaps you can help me right now. There's one man in particular I'd like to speak to. His name is Horace Putney. Do you know him?"

"Oh, sure. I think he's in the dining room right now. Would you like me to introduce you?"

Krakin thought for a moment. "I don't want to interrupt him. I'll call on him later. Do you know his room number?"

"Sure." Andrews pulled a sheet of paper out of his pocket. "Room 325."

"Thank you. I'll go on up to my room now. I hope I'll see you later. Maybe I can buy you a drink, to repay you for your help."

"I'd like that. Nice to meet you."

16

Krakin deposited his G.U.M. plastic and cardboard suitcase in his room and washed his face. He was hungry, but he decided to wait a little longer for dinner. On the table in his room he noticed a small pile of postcards. He had never had postcards in a hotel room before. Probably the manager brought them out when there was a large contingent of foreign visitors. Unable to resist the temptation, he took one and addressed it to Anya. "Having a wonderful time in Leningrad," he wrote on the back. "Just seeing this beautiful city and its hard working, efficient people fills one with pride over the accomplishments of socialism." Krakin smiled to himself as he signed his name. Let's see what the KGB does with *that*, he thought.

Krakin went back downstairs. He bought some stamps at the kiosk, put one on the postcard, and dropped it in the hotel mailbox. Then he went into the restaurant. The crowd was thinning out and he was seated promptly, but that was the only speedy thing about the meal. The fish Krakin ordered was overcooked and tasteless, and the wine he drank with it was worse. He didn't even half-finish the carafe.

When the meal finally ended, it was after nine-thirty. Krakin decided to go directly up to Putney's room. He did, and knocked firmly on the door. It opened promptly and Krakin faced a tall, spare man with an almost totally bald head and deep wrinkles and age spots on his face. Krakin guessed the man must be close to seventy.

"Yes?" Putney said, in English.

Krakin reached back into his memory of secondary school language courses. He had studied English extensively, and read British and American periodicals occasionally to keep up his familiarity with it, but he hadn't conversed in it for some time. "My name is Leo Krakin," he said haltingly. "I'm a journalist with the magazine published by the Party organization in the Basilgrad Region. I would like to talk with you in preparation for an article about Western literature."

Putney looked at his watch. "It's rather late," he said. "Can't we do this tomorrow?" Just from this little snatch of conversation, Krakin could see that Putney was a tough, humorless old goat, with a strong sense of his own self-importance.

"I can also tell you about some things that may interest you in Basilgrad." Krakin tried to adopt an I-know-something-you-don't-know expression. Putney looked at him curiously for a moment, then let him into the room.

"This is a nice room," Krakin said. "I certainly appreciate your help with my article." While he spoke he walked to the sink that stood on the other side of the room. He turned the water on full force, then beckoned Putney to come near him.

"Your manuscript has been lost. I'm trying to find it. I need information from you." Krakin spoke in a quieter voice.

"Why are we over here? Why did you turn on the water?"

"To avoid the listening devices. I don't know where they are, and even if I found them I couldn't shut them off without the listeners knowing about it."

Putney seemed to understand perfectly. He apparently had concluded that Krakin might have something significant to say. "What's this about a manuscript?"

"The Polokov book. You know what I'm talking about?"

Putney nodded. The man was decisive. "I'm going to buy it from him when we get to Basilgrad."

"Not unless I find it. It's missing. I think someone has stolen it."

"What?"

"It may be the KGB, but I'm not sure. I have several people in mind, but I need to know from you the names of everyone--and I mean everyone--who knows you want to buy the book."

"Who are you?"

"I work for Polokov. I suppose in the United States I would be called a 'private detective.' "

"How do I know you work for Polokov?"

"You'll have to trust me. Besides, I'm not asking for anything that would be harmful if I'm not what I say I am."

"Unless you're with the police yourself."

"On that you'll have to believe me. I can only say that the socialist police do not very often obtain information this way. They have other methods."

"Yes. All right. I believe you. But I can't help you. The only person I ever told was that messenger I sent. Tvori was his name. I haven't mentioned it to any of the other publishers, for obvious reasons."

"Are you sure you told no one else?"

"Positive. This is a very confidential matter, Mr. Krakin."

"Could Tvori have told anyone?"

Putney shrugged. "I instructed him not to."

"Who is this Tvori? What do you know about him?"

"Not much."

"How do you know him?"

"He was recommended to me as a trustworthy courier."

"By whom?"

"A friend."

"Who?" Krakin was insistent.

"Must you know?"

"Do you want to buy that manuscript?"

"His name is Andrews. He's a news correspondent here. He's been making the arrangements for us in Leningrad."

"I'll be damned."

"I beg your pardon."

"I've already met him. He helped me check in. Can he find Tvori?"

"If he can't, I don't know who can."

Krakin stared into Putney's stony face. "Is there anything else that you can think of that might be helpful?"

Putney shook his head.

"You're sure you told no one else?"

"Yes."

"How did you know that Polokov had a book?"

"I didn't until Tvori found out for me. I learned about Polokov's work through rumors in the American scientific community. I'm rather proud of ferreting the thing out."

Krakin thought for a moment and then reached over and shut off the water. He walked back to the center of the room. "Well," he said, "I do appreciate your willingness to help me, and I'm awfully sorry to have called on you so late. Can we meet again tomorrow? Say for lunch?"

"We've got a pretty busy schedule tomorrow. Tours and meetings."

"Perhaps we could breakfast together. I'm staying at the hotel, too. I plan to do quite a bit of work yet tonight, and we could discuss it in the morning."

"I'll meet you in the hotel restaurant at eight."

"Thank you, Mr. Putney. I'll see you then." Krakin shook hands with Putney and left the room.

<h2 style="text-align:center">17</h2>

No point in wasting time waiting around until tomorrow, Krakin thought. If Andrews is in, he might be able to get to Tvori yet tonight. Krakin walked up to the fourth floor on the ornate staircase, a bourgeois vestige from pre-revolutionary days, left intact by the administration only because most guests used the modern elevator which had been installed in the building.

Krakin remembered that Andrews had said he was in room 402. He stopped in front of that door and knocked. No answer. Perhaps it was a different room. Krakin debated what to do. He could go ask the woman on the floor who kept the keys, but he didn't think it was a good idea to be identified with a suspicious Westerner any more than necessary.

Just then the elevator door at the far end of the corridor opened. Andrews emerged and walked toward Krakin. Krakin went to greet him.

"Hello," Krakin said. I was just looking for you. I'm afraid I need to ask you for another favor." Krakin was glad to be able to revert to Russian.

"I hope maybe you were looking for me to buy me that drink."

"Oh, I'll get around to that, I promise. But right now I need some information. Can we talk?"

"Sure." Andrews opened the door to his room and they both went in. Krakin headed immediately for the sink and turned on the water.

Andrews came up behind him and turned the water off. "No need for that," he said with a smile. "Look." He stepped to the far wall and carefully took down one of the pictures. A microphone was imbedded in the back, but a wire leading from it into the wall had been cut.

"How did you do that without tipping them off?" Krakin asked.

"There are ways. An American living in this country has to find them out, believe me. Now, what can I help you with?"

"I've been to see Putney. He tells me that a little less than a week ago he needed a confidential messenger to go to Basilgrad. You found someone for him, a man named Tvori."

"That's right. But I don't quite see what this has to do with that article you're going to write."

"It doesn't. But what I'm doing is in Putney's interest as well as my own. You can check with him if you like."

Andrews looked at Krakin for a moment. "I will, eventually. What is it you want from me?"

"I want to find Tvori and speak with him. As soon as possible."

"Sure. I think I know where he is. When do you want to see

him?"

"Tonight. I don't have much time."

Andrews considered. "All right. I'll take you there."

Krakin hesitated. Under the circumstances, he really didn't want to be seen traveling with a Westerner, though he welcomed Andrews' help. "I appreciate your offer, but I'm sure I can find him myself. Just tell me where he is."

"You'll never find the place by yourself, believe me. And I've got a car. The trains and taxis stop running here at twelve, so you won't be able to get there and back tonight without me."

Andrews did have a point. Krakin had been stranded before, in Basilgrad, when the transportation system shut down for the night. "All right. Are you ready to go now?"

"I think perhaps I'd better clear this with Putney. And I've got one other person to see this evening. How about I meet you in the lobby in half an hour?"

Krakin agreed and went downstairs to wait.

18

Andrews finally came down to the lobby at ten thirty. Krakin was reading a newspaper and didn't see him at first. "Well, Mr. Krakin, I'm available any time for that drink you offered me," Andrews said, for the benefit of anyone who happened to be listening.

Krakin looked up. He was confused for a moment, then caught on. "Sure. I guess I can't go back on my word." He got up. "Shall we step into the bar?"

"Tell you what. I know a little place over near the Theater Square. Very nice atmosphere. Why don't we go there? We can even take my car."

"Affluent American. Naturally I dislike such luxury, but since

I'm in your debt, I must accept."

They went outside. The wind had picked up and was swirling papers around on the relatively quiet street. Krakin pulled up the collar of his suit jacket and wished he had taken the time to go back up to his room to get his coat. Andrews' car was parked on a street just off the Nevsky Prospekt about a block away. It was the small, ugly Moskvitch sedan that cost the equivalent of three years of Krakin's salary. He had hoped that Andrews would own one of the sporty Western cars that he occasionally saw being driven in Basilgrad. Krakin had never been inside a Western car.

"My employer owns this," Andrews said, half-apologetically, after they had climbed inside the car and Andrews had managed to get it started. "They feel it's necessary for certain kinds of news coverage. I'm not allowed to take it outside of Leningrad without special permission."

Krakin nodded. After letting the motor run another minute, Andrews put it in gear and they moved haltingly out into the street. Andrews took them to the Nevsky Prospekt and turned west.

"Did you talk to Putney?" Krakin asked.

"Yep."

"What did he tell you?"

"That you're okay. That I should help you."

Andrews turned left. They drove down toward Theater Square.

"Did he tell you anything else?"

"Yep."

"Like what?"

Andrews glanced over toward Krakin, then back to the road. "Pretty much everything, I guess. About Polokov. And the manuscript that you're looking for."

"You don't mind getting involved in it?"

"I'm not getting involved. I'm just helping out a fellow countryman. Putney is a pretty big deal back home, you know. He wants that manuscript more than you do."

"I appreciate your help."

Krakin settled back and looked out the window. The cold

inhibited further conversation. They went past Theater Square and continued on south. Krakin kept waiting for the car's heater to start working, but it never did. A few kilometers past Theater Square Andrews turned off into a narrow, crooked side street. He wove the car through a network of small alleyways, some scarcely wide enough to permit the car to pass.

"You see," Andrews said, "you would have had trouble finding this yourself."

At last they stopped in front of a dark, rundown wooden building. In pre-Revolutionary times it was probably the modest residence of a middle-class merchant. Now, Krakin could see as he and Andrews stood outside, it had been divided into several apartments, probably not much bigger than single rooms.

"Tvori is on the first floor," Andrews said.

"Thanks. No need for you to come up if you'd rather wait here. I shouldn't be too long."

"Oh, I'll come. I know Tvori slightly. Maybe he'll be more cooperative if he knows you're with me."

"Suit yourself."

They went inside. The tiny hallway smelled of burning coal and cooking grease, but at least it was warm. Krakin started up the stairs first. There was no lamp, and practically no light filtered in through the single dirty window at the top of the stairs. Krakin began to feel uncomfortable. He had a sudden urge to turn around and go back to the hotel. Why did he need to talk to Tvori, anyway? But he continued on, tense and slightly fearful. Andrews' presence close behind him gave him little support; Krakin was now aware of him as an obstacle to retreat.

Krakin came to a tiny hallway with two doors. One was slightly ajar and appeared to open into a room above the ground floor hall. He pushed it further open. It smelled like a bathroom. The other door then must lead to Tvori's flat. Krakin knocked. The loudness of it in the still house startled him. He exchanged glances with Andrews.

A shuffling noise came from inside. After a bit the door opened slightly and a face appeared, silhouetted against the dim light coming from the room behind. It was a round face, unshaven, with deep lines. The head was balding, and a spot on it shone in the light from inside.

"Who is it?" the face asked. A heavy cloud of alcoholic breath accompanied the words.

"My name is Leo Krakin. I'm from Basilgrad. Professor Polokov sent me to see you. It's about his book."

"Polokov? What does he want?" The man's speech was indistinct, but comprehensible. He had a trace of a rural accent on top of the slurring. As he spoke he appeared to notice Andrews for the first time. Andrews was now standing close behind Krakin. "Is there someone with you?" Tvori asked.

"Yes," Andrews said. "I'm Steve Andrews. You should remember me. You've done some jobs for me from time to time. I'm with the International Press."

"I remember. Is this man with you?" Tvori nodded toward Krakin.

"Yes. He is. I brought him here to see you."

Slowly Tvori pulled the door open. He stepped back quickly--a little too quickly, Krakin thought. Tvori had his right hand behind his back.

Krakin moved gingerly into the room. His nerve ends tingled. Something was wrong. Something about Tvori.

Then it came. Tvori lunged forward at Krakin. His hand emerged from behind his back and the dull silver blade of a long knife sprouted from it.

Krakin stepped backward, hard, at the first suggestion of Tvori's movement. He knew Andrews would be there, blocking his way, not realizing what was happening, so he lowered his shoulder and threw his energy into it. He hit the American in the chest and Andrews tumbled backward down the stairs.

Krakin had no time to look after his friend. He had escaped Tvori's first strike, but now he was standing defenseless in the tiny hallway as Tvori came at him again.

This time Krakin sidestepped, his side banging against the

bathroom door. Tvori was slow. The alcoholic haze that surrounded him was real. Krakin reached out and grabbed Tvori's knife arm with both of his hands. The man's forearm was like a small tree trunk, but Krakin managed to slam the hand into the wall. He did it again. Tvori howled and tried to turn and reach for Krakin's head with his other hand, but he stumbled and half fell. The knife dropped from his grasp. Krakin pulled the man up and twisted his arm behind his back. Tvori was panting heavily.

"Now get inside," Krakin growled, pulling even harder on Tvori's arm, pushing his body back toward his room.

Suddenly, unexpectedly, two quick flashes of light, accompanied by soft bursting sounds came from down the stairs. The body Krakin was holding tensed briefly, then went limp. The resistance went out of the strong arm; it felt lifeless.

Krakin gradually released his hold, then let go. Tvori's body sagged onto the floor of the hall. Krakin heard Andrews coming back up the stairs. The light from Tvori's room glinted on a dark metal object in Andrews' hand.

"You shot him! For Christ's sake, you shot him," Krakin exclaimed.

"What the hell did you expect me to do? Lie down there and watch him cut you into little pieces?"

"I already had the knife out of his hand. I was taking him back to his room. He was too drunk to resist. Couldn't you see that?"

"Damn it, all I saw was the knife. Then you knocked me down the stairs." He rubbed his arm. "You're a lot tougher than you look."

"Help me get him back into his room," Krakin said. "Christ, he's bleeding all over the place." Krakin was angry. Tvori wasn't going to answer any questions now, and how were they going to explain this to the police? But he held his tongue. After all, Andrews had acted to save Krakin's life. Or so it seemed.

"We can't put him there. We've got to get rid of him." Andrews went inside Tvori's room for a moment and came out with a couple of old rags. One he stuffed inside Tvori's shirt. The other he used to wipe the blood off the floor. Then he stuffed it inside Tvori's shirt as well. "The bleeding's just about stopped. We can move him outside in a minute."

Krakin watched all this open-mouthed. Andrews acted as if he were just mopping up a spilled bottle of wine. Krakin had the impression that Andrews had done this sort of thing before. "What do you mean, move him outside?" Krakin finally said. "You're not suggesting that we don't report this?"

"You're damn right I am. You ought to know what happens to an American who gets involved in something like this."

"But you did it to save my life. The guy was attacking me. I'll tell them that."

Andrews shook his head. "They'll believe what they want to, not what you tell them. Krakin, I just can't take the chance."

Krakin considered. What was the risk to him? "Well, you do what you want to with him. You shot him. By the way, where the hell did you get a gun? Christ, you can get sent away just for having that."

"Now you see why we can't report this. As for the gun, obviously I brought it with me. Where I come from, a man has a right to keep a gun for self-defense. God knows there's plenty of need for self-defense over here."

"But a gun with a silencer? You need *that* for self-defense?"

Andrews shrugged. "Come on, let's get this guy down to my car. I think he'll fit in the trunk."

"'Not until after I search his room."

"What? We don't have time for that."

"Then carry him out yourself. I'm going to see if he had that manuscript. That's what I came here for."

"You're a fool. We can get caught."

"I don't care."

"Oh, all right. But at least help me move him inside while you look."

They carried Tvori's body into his room. While Andrews did another clean-up job and bandaged Tvori's wounds, Krakin searched. The place was filthy, but Tvori had little furniture and few other possessions, so there wasn't much to go through. After ten minutes

Krakin was satisfied that the manuscript wasn't in Tvori's room. Krakin stopped looking and leaned against the wall to scratch his head and think.

"Are you finished?" Andrews asked.

"Damn it. He's got to have the thing. Why else would he have attacked me?"

"He was drunk. May be thought you were a burglar."

"I told him who I was. And he saw you. That's when he attacked me." Krakin looked at Andrews. "What's your relationship with Tvori anyway? What do you know about him?"

"Nothing that's going to help you here. I'll tell you what I know in the car. Now let's get him down there."

Krakin took one last glance around Tvori's room. Then they carried his body downstairs, closing his door behind them. There was no lock.

The darkness concealed them as they carried Tvori to the car and stuffed him into the trunk. It was a tight fit. When they finished they were both sweating, although the night was still cold and windy.

In the car on the way back to the hotel Krakin repeated his questions about Tvori.

"I really don't know much about him," Andrews answered. "He was recommended to me by the guy I replaced here a year and a half ago. He's done courier jobs for me four or five times--you know, where you don't dare send something through the mail. He's always been trustworthy."

"Didn't he have a job?"

"As I understand it, he used to be a railroad laborer, but he got hurt somehow and was retired with a small pension. He's about fifty. Lived alone there."

"No family?"

"None that I know of, but he wasn't exactly a close friend." Andrews paused. "Say, you're not going to start investigating him, are you?"

"I've got to find out if he had that manuscript."

"Krakin, why don't you give up? You're going to make trouble for yourself. And for me."

"I'll be careful."

"You'd better just leave this alone, Krakin." Andrews' words were very serious. It almost sounded as if they carried a threat.

Krakin didn't answer. He stared forward out the car's window into the black night. The events of the evening were beginning to have their full impact on him. He had almost been killed. He had been a party to a killing. His whole life could be wrecked by what had happened tonight. He thought of Anya. God, how he missed her. All he wanted now was to go home to her, to forget about all this mess.

Andrews pulled up in front of the Neva. "Get out," he said. "I'll see you later."

"What are you going to do with Tvori?"

"Don't worry. I'll get rid of him. You hang around. I want to talk with you when I get back."

"Where would I go? Out to a night club?" Krakin got out of the car. He watched as Andrews sped away. Then he went up to his room. His hand was shaking. He looked through his suitcase for his bottle of vodka and took a long drink.

Krakin just wanted to lie down and go to sleep, to forget the evening. But there was something he had to do. He drew some paper out of his writing folder, picked up a pen, and began to write. He worked for twenty minutes, covering both sides of several sheets. Then he took a hotel envelope out of his table drawer, put the pages inside, and sealed it. He went out of his room into the hall. Five minutes later he was back, without the envelope. He took another long drink of vodka, then removed his shoes, lay back on his bed, and thought about Anya.

After what seemed like just a few minutes, a sharp knock sounded on the door of Krakin's room. Andrews again, thought Krakin. He knew what Andrews was going to say, but he didn't want to hear it. The knock came again. Slowly Krakin rose, went to the door, and opened it. He stood face-to-face with three hard-looking men in gray overcoats. He had never seen any of them before, but there was no doubt in his mind who they were.

"Leo Krakin?" the nearest one asked. Without waiting for an answer, he went on. "We're from the KGB. You're to come with us. I would suggest that you bring your things with you. It will be a while before you can return."

19

Krakin picked up his belongings in silence and then followed two of the three men out to a waiting car--a big, black Zil sedan-- where a fourth man waited behind the wheel. One of the men remained in Krakin's room, doubtless to conduct a thorough search. The car moved away as soon as they were inside. No one spoke. To Krakin's surprise, they headed straight down the Nevsky Prospekt to the Moscow Station, passed it, then turned into an alleyway that ran alongside and under the station platforms. Surely they didn't mean to work him over or kill him down here. Common thugs would do that, but not the KGB.

The car stopped near the end of a platform.

"Get out, please," the man sitting next to Krakin in the back seat said. He wasn't polite, but he wasn't exactly nasty either. He had bushy eyebrows and a fat face. He looked a bit older than the others and acted as if an abduction in the middle of the night was a routine event, which maybe for him it was.

Krakin got out. He thought momentarily of running away, but immediately rejected the thought. He had come close enough to a bullet already this evening. The two men from the hotel also got out, and the car drove away. The men led Krakin, carrying his suitcase and writing folder, which he had never had a chance to put away, underneath the station platform. There were no lights here, and the heavy concrete pillars supporting the tracks cut off most of the light from the streetlamps adjacent to the platform. Krakin felt himself beginning to shiver again, not entirely from the cold.

They stopped abruptly before what, in the dim light, appeared to be a small, soot-blackened frame maintenance shed amid the forest of thick pillars. The younger man who had been in the front seat of the car fumbled for a key, then opened a door in the shed and turned on a light inside. It wasn't a maintenance building at all, but a stairway leading up to the platform. Krakin went up the stairs between the men.

They emerged from the stairway into a small, concrete-block structure which, Krakin could see through the single window, sat at the end of one of the train platforms. "Wait here," the younger man said. He unlocked another door and went out onto the platform. Krakin and the other man passed the time staring at each other in silence.

A few minutes later the man who had left returned. "It's all ready," he said. The three of them went onto the platform and walked about fifty yards until they came to a single railway car sitting on the track. It appeared to be a standard passenger car, but Krakin couldn't see into any of the windows.

"All right, let's go inside." The younger man reached out and swung open the door at the end of the car. A shaft of light shone through the opening. They entered. At once Krakin could see that this was no ordinary passenger carrier. The walls inside were all bright, shiny metal, and there were large, heavy locks on each of the compartment doors.

"Wait here," said the man who had opened the door. He went ahead as Krakin and the older agent with the bushy eyebrows stood in the center passageway.

"What is this place?" Krakin asked. These were the first words he had spoken since the KGB agents appeared at his hotel room door.

"This is what we use to transport sensitive personnel. No one can break in. Or out."

"What's your name?" Krakin asked. Having broken his silence once, he might as well be communicative.

"Karl."

"Well, Karl, what do you want of me? Is there a torture

chamber here to put me in? Don't bother, I haven't any secrets."

Karl laughed. It sounded like an axe on concrete. "We're just a transportation unit. They don't tell us about anything else."

"Then where are you transporting me?"

"You'll find out soon enough,"

Krakin put down his bag and held out his writing folder. "Look, I'm a writer for the *Party Organ* in Basilgrad. Here's the article I've been working on here. Read it. Maybe it's the information the KGB wants. It sets out my most serious thoughts."

Karl reached out and firmly pushed the folder back at Krakin. "That's not my job," he said. "That's up to Interrogation."

The younger agent returned down the passageway, a large set of keys clinking in his hand. He stopped at a compartment door near Krakin, unlocked and opened it. "Here you are, Comrade Krakin. You'll ride here."

Krakin stood still. "For how long? Where are we going? I don't want to be cooped up in there."

"You'll stay here for the rest of the night. You'll find a comfortable bed and a lavatory inside. We'll have breakfast for you in the morning, after we're underway."

"If you don't want to rest," Karl added, "perhaps you can do some more writing. Perhaps it will make the work of Interrogation easier, no?" Karl laughed again. The sound set Krakin's teeth on edge. He picked up his bag and went inside the compartment. The door slammed shut behind him, making a very solid sound.

Krakin inspected the inside of the compartment. Half of one seat had been removed, on the side away from the window, for the installation of a toilet and sink. Steel bars were bolted over the window. Otherwise, it seemed of ordinary construction, but Krakin knew that it had been carefully designed to prevent either escape or suicide.

Not that he was contemplating either. In his circumstances, they were roughly equivalent. No, he would have to let the events carry him to their conclusion. Perhaps in the process he would solve the mystery of the missing manuscript. Satisfied that there was nothing further he could do now, he turned off the light and stretched out on the unaltered seat. It had been a long, hard day, and a great deal had happened.

20

The swaying of the car woke Krakin. He opened his eyes slowly, unsure of his surroundings. It took only a glance to remind him where he was.

Krakin sat up. There was light coming in the window. He inspected it. Behind the steel bars was a thick translucent sheet of glass or plastic. It allowed light to enter, but permitted no view of what was on the other side. Krakin leaned back on the seat. He wondered why the KGB had brought him here, instead of to their Leningrad offices. Surely they had competent interrogators in Leningrad. But perhaps this case lay within the jurisdiction of the Basilgrad office, since it had originated there. The bureaucracies were well known to be jealous of their authority and the KGB was probably no exception. Basilgrad must be where they were taking him. A day earlier than he expected, but he could use the extra time.

Half an hour passed. Krakin could sense that the train was moving rapidly; they must be well into the open country. The light was even stronger. The sun must be up by now, Krakin thought.

A key scratched on the metal lock of Krakin's door. Slowly and cautiously the door opened. It was Karl, carrying a steaming tray. The food on it smelled surprisingly good.

"Here's your breakfast," Karl said in his gravelly voice. "Hope you're having a pleasant trip."

"I'm especially enjoying the view," Krakin replied, then regretted it as Karl began to laugh.

"We apologize for that. There's really no reason for you not to see out, but all the security compartments have the frosted windows."

"Why don't you put me in an insecure compartment? I'm not going to run away."

"We have our orders." Karl put the tray down on the short seat. "Just bang on the wall when you're finished. I'll come get the tray." He started to leave.

"Where are we going? Basilgrad?"

Karl smiled. "You'll see."

"Surely you can tell me that."

Karl shook his head. "I can't. Orders. But I'll tell you this much: we don't expect to get there till tomorrow morning, so you'll have another chance at that breakfast if you don't finish it this morning."

Tomorrow morning! But Basilgrad was only ten hours away. Krakin's first thought was of Polokov's manuscript. Today was Thursday, and the Western publishers would be flying home on Sunday evening. By the time he got back to Basilgrad, they might have come and gone. But concern over the manuscript faded to nothing in the light of Krakin's second thought. By tomorrow morning the train could easily reach a place from which he might never return. He had a strong foreboding of what their unknown destination might be.

21

The last Czar of all the Russias, Nicholas II, and his family were murdered in July, 1918, in a city on the eastern slope of the Urals then known as Yekaterinburg. The name did not long survive the victims. Like everything else it too changed to conform to the new order: the city now bore the name of the man who engineered the Czar's murder.

In the decades that followed the city became, among other

things, a stopping-off point for the thousands of prisoners bound for the mines and smelters of the Urals. Krakin had always believed, though with little hard evidence, that this was where his father had gone when they took him away in the spring of 1933. A realist, Krakin had never held out the hope that some day he and his father would be reunited. Prisoners taken to the mining camps in the 1930s simply did not return. Not ever.

As Krakin stepped down from the train the next morning onto the wooden platform, he wondered if indeed he was not following in his father's footsteps, notwithstanding the changes in the U.S.S.R. of the past decade. He saw nothing to allay his fears. Rather, the distant city in the valley below him, its snow-covered rooftops, its grid-like streets, and the heavy industrial smoke that filled the air even on this brisk morning merely confirmed his suspicions.

"Sverdlovsk," Krakin said to Karl, who stood at his elbow. The younger KGB man had gone off into a little wooden building at the end of the platform. The car in which Krakin had traveled from Leningrad was sitting on a siding next to the platform. The locomotive that had brought them here to the hills just west of the city could still be seen continuing eastward down into the valley. The morning sun glinted off the small frozen lakes that interspersed the city's grid.

Karl just looked at Krakin and grinned.

After a short time the other man emerged from the building. "They're on their way," he told Karl. The three of them then waited wordlessly on the platform, the two KGB men watching the dirt road, recently plowed, that led off to the north from the platform and disappeared behind a hill.

Krakin was surprised at the vehicle which ground up to meet them fifteen minutes later. It wasn't the big, black sedan he had expected but an Army truck, with large red stars emblazoned on its sides and hood. Once underway, Krakin could see why the truck was necessary. No car could have got through the drifts they encountered back in the hills.

As they climbed north into the Urals, Krakin tried to get hold of himself. Surely, he thought, the KGB wouldn't go to all this trouble, with special guards and a special railroad car, just to deposit him in a labor camp. His fears weren't rational. They were based on memories of a different time. Stalin was dead. Beria was long gone. Even if the labor camps still existed, one had to be tried and convicted before being sent away, even if the trial was but a formality. They wouldn't just take him away to a camp without even placing any charges against him. Or would they? What other explanation could there be for bringing him here? Would he never see Anya again? Would she even know what had happened to him?

The truck continued on up the winding road, occasionally slipping and sliding in the deep snow. An hour passed without any communication among the men in the truck. Sverdlovsk and all signs of civilization were well behind them. Then, as the truck rounded the side of a hill, an unexpected sight confronted Krakin. Stretched out below them, in a long narrow valley between two high hills, lay a huge cluster of buildings, of all sizes and shapes. They filled an area of the valley more than a kilometer long. At first glance the fears that Krakin had just rationalized away returned. But, on further inspection, he noted discrepancies between the complex of buildings and his mental image of a labor camp. There was nothing that looked like barracks. The buildings were all new. It wasn't a mining camp. It looked more like a cross between a modern factory and a new university. Still afraid, still expecting the worst, Krakin allowed himself a ray of hope.

The truck turned off the main road onto a narrower gravel road that descended toward the buildings. After a few minutes they stopped at a gate set in the high metal fence that appeared to surround the complex. A guard, in Army uniform, inspected the contents of the truck, then waved the driver on through. They followed a narrow roadway that threaded among the buildings. Well into the center of the enclave, the truck stopped again.

"This is it, Comrade." Karl said. "We're here."

"You didn't have to go to all this trouble. Really."

Karl didn't laugh. A sergeant and a corporal came out of the large, windowless cube of a building near them. They saluted. Karl and his companion casually returned the salute.

"Leo Krakin?" the sergeant asked.

"That's me," Krakin answered, getting out of the truck. Karl handed Krakin his suitcase and his writing folder.

"Here's your papers," Karl said. "I hope the colonel likes them." This time he did laugh.

The driver put the truck in gear. Krakin watched as it slowly drove away.

22

The two soldiers led Krakin into the building and up to the first floor. It was brightly lit and antiseptic looking. Almost like a hospital. It even smelled like a hospital, Krakin noticed. A knot of fear formed and re-formed in his stomach. He determined to ignore it.

"In here, please." The sergeant opened a door and directed Krakin inside. His manner was peculiar. His statement was half an order, half a request.

Krakin went into a white-walled room, about five meters square, empty except for a table and some wooden chairs. Almost as soon as he was inside, another door, opposite the one through which Krakin had entered, opened and two men, one in an Army uniform and the other in a gray suit, came in. A third man, in a sergeant's uniform, followed and stood by the door. The latter held a rifle and looked as though he wouldn't hesitate to use it.

"Leo Krakin, I believe," said the man in the gray suit. He looked a lot like Karl, but older and more clever. It wasn't difficult to guess his occupation. "My name is Varkov. This is Colonel Tarygin." He nodded toward the uniformed man who, unlike Varkov, had a thin, but straight, body and a narrow, almost aristocratic face. The Colonel came from a long line of Army officers as surely as Varkov came from solid peasant stock. Krakin wondered who had authority over the other now. He would bet ten-to-one on Varkov.

"Please sit down, Comrade Krakin," Varkov said. Krakin sat down at one side of the table; the others sat at the opposite side.

"Tell me," Krakin said, "why you've gone to all the trouble of bringing me here. Was it my postcard?"

"Postcard?" Varkov asked, his dark eyebrows descending momentarily. "Oh, that." He smiled. "No, we've been watching you for much longer than that. Ever since you asked Comrade Mekorian to get secret KGB information for you." He shook his head. "You shouldn't have done that."

"What about her? Is she all right?"

Varkov raised his eyebrows. "You don't deny asking her to spy for you?"

"I don't deny that I asked her to look at a file on a certain person. I do deny that I did anything against the interest of the State."

"That, Comrade Krakin, is for us to decide."

"Is she all right?"

"I believe so. She made a mistake, but not so bad a mistake as you made." Varkov waved his hand to dismiss further conversation about Krakin's unfortunate accomplice. "Now then, Krakin," Varkov continued, "we have investigated you very carefully. You are an interesting, clever man. But you won't be able to keep anything from us."

"I don't intend to."

"Please, Krakin, don't interrupt me." Varkov looked down at a sheet of paper he placed on the table. "You were born in 1923, in Gorki. You grew up there. Your father was a Party member, but in 1933 he was arrested for crimes against the State."

"He wasn't guilty."

"Perhaps he was. Perhaps he wasn't. Nevertheless he was sent away and appears to be dead. After the arrest your family moved to Moscow to live with an uncle. You went to the university in Moscow but did not join the Komsomol." Varkov's eyebrows went up again and he looked at Krakin, then back at the paper. "You studied journalism and when you graduated you began your service with the Army. Somehow you managed to spend most of the war in Moscow, writing propaganda bulletins," Varkov shook his head in disgust. "After the war you worked for the State Publishing Company in Moscow. In 1953 you went to Basilgrad, where you now live. You work for the *Party Organ*, even though you aren't a Party member."

Varkov lifted his head again. "A rather questionable background, I'd say." He looked at the Colonel.

"You didn't mention my library fines," Krakin said.

"You won't be so flippant when we've finished, Comrade." Varkov went back to his paper. "We know, Krakin, that for several years now you have engaged in activities outside your regular employment. Conducting a writers group. Doing investigations for people. Generally showing a complete disregard for your regular work."

"Have you asked my Chief Editor about that?"

"Please, Krakin, don't interrupt me."

Colonel Tarygin looked at Varkov and spoke for the first time, in a quiet, authoritative voice. "What does his editor say, Varkov?" Krakin realized that he apparently had underestimated the Colonel.

"He had no complaints. Obviously this fellow has him fooled. No one can do so many things and still fulfill his plan." Varkov was arguing.

"Hmm," said the Colonel. He turned back to Krakin. Could it be, Krakin asked himself, that the KGB man was actually taking orders from the Colonel? Or was this just a trick of interrogation?

"To continue," Varkov said, "you have a soft young girlfriend in Basilgrad who misses you." Varkov grinned evilly. "You are employed in an investigation by Professor Polokov of Basilgrad University concerning a certain manuscript, and you spent the evening before last in the company of an American agent." Varkov placed his hands on the table, palms up. "So you see, Comrade Krakin, we know a great deal about you. We will know if you are not telling us the truth. So please, let us begin. What were you doing in Leningrad?"

Krakin shrugged and tried to appear candid. "Looking for the manuscript you mentioned. And preparing an article for my magazine. Would you like to see the draft? I have it right here."

Varkov ignored the question. "Did you find the manuscript?"

"No."

"Why did you think the manuscript was in Leningrad?"

"Polokov told me that one of the Western publishers visiting Leningrad knew about it. I thought the publisher might have told others about it."

"What's this publisher's name?"

"Putney. Horace Putney."

"Did you talk with him?"

"Yes."

"Well, had he talked to others about the manuscript?"

Krakin hesitated. "No one except a man he sent to Basilgrad to ask Polokov about the manuscript."

"He mentioned no one else?"

"No one."

"What's this messenger's name?"

"Tvori. Laszlo Tvori."

"Did you talk to Tvori about the manuscript?"

"No." Krakin was treading on thin ice here. He didn't himself know how he was going to handle questions about Tvori.

"Ask him about the American agent," the colonel said.

"Yes, what were you doing yesterday evening with the American correspondent, the man named Andrews?"

"Well, I first met him quite by accident when I checked into the hotel in Leningrad. The clerk had lost my reservation, but Andrews stepped up to remind the clerk that there were still empty rooms in the hotel." A smile flickered across the colonel's face. "Later, Putney told me that Andrews knew how to get in touch with Tvori, so I asked Andrews to help me find him."

"You were seen going off in Andrews' car late Wednesday night," Varkov said accusingly.

"Andrews showed me where Tvori lived, then we came back

to the hotel."

"You say you didn't talk to Tvori. Did you see him?"

Krakin hesitated again. Should he tell the truth? How much did they already know? "Yes. I saw him."

"Well, why didn't he talk to you?"

"Just a minute, Varkov," the colonel interrupted. "We don't need all these details. You can save that for your routine interrogations." The colonel turned to Krakin. Were they playing games with him, Krakin wondered. And why wasn't this a "routine" interrogation?

"Tell me, Krakin," the colonel continued, "do you believe that Tvori has this manuscript?"

"No. I'm fairly sure he doesn't."

"Then who do you think does?"

"Until you and your friend started asking me questions this morning, I thought perhaps the KGB did."

"Does it?" the colonel snapped at Varkov.

"Of course not," Varkov replied.

"Who else do you suspect?" the colonel asked Krakin.

"Well, there are two students who work for Polokov. I had thought they were reporting to the KGB, but . . ." Krakin looked at Varkov, whose face was blank.

"They're not working for the KGB," the colonel replied. "They're working for me. And they don't have the manuscript." The colonel paused. "Comrade Krakin, do you have the manuscript?"

"No, I've never seen it."

"All right. Let me ask you another question, to which I demand a direct and complete answer. Do you know why Polokov hired you to find the manuscript?"

There was no avoiding this one. " I believe he hoped to sell it to Putney for publication in the West."

The colonel seemed to relax. "That's what we thought, but I wanted to be sure. Now, please tell me, who else do you suspect might have Polokov's book?"

"All I can do is tell you the possibilities I've considered.

Perhaps Polokov's wife hid it. I've talked to her and she's very much afraid of what will happen if the book is published. But I don't think she did it. Perhaps a jealous colleague stole it, but as far as I know Polokov's colleagues don't even know about the manuscript. It could just be someone who thought he could sell the manuscript, but I doubt it. I've checked that theory with certain people who ought to know, and they tell me the book wasn't stolen by a professional. They're still looking into it, though."

"You checked with your friend Peter Solin, you mean," Varkov said with a triumphant smile.

"I checked with Solin, but I don't consider him a friend."

"Go on. Go on, please," said the colonel impatiently, giving Varkov a cold glance. "Who else?"

"The only other possibility is someone Polokov mentioned, an important man who Polokov thinks would not want the book published for professional reasons."

"Who is that?"

"The man's name is Lysenko. I understand he's the President of the Lenin Academy of Agricultural Science." Krakin hadn't told Colonel Tarygin quite everything, but this seemed a good place to stop. He had the feeling it might be dangerous to exhaust his entire supply of information.

The Colonel sat open-mouthed, obviously taken aback at Krakin's last statement. "That's it?" he finally asked. "That's everyone?"

"Yes."

The colonel ran his fingers through his hair and then slumped back in his chair. "Well, at least you've found out more than the KGB."

Varkov looked unhappy. Krakin was aware of a subtle--or perhaps not so subtle--change in the atmosphere. It was apparent that he had not been brought here solely because he was suspected of crimes against the State.

"I still think I could find the manuscript, if I had time," Krakin ventured hopefully, testing the wind.

"You do?" The colonel brightened.

"Yes, but I can't do it here. I need to get back to work before the publishers leave. They're scheduled to depart from Basilgrad on Sunday evening."

"But today is Friday." The colonel was biting.

"Then I can't stay here long."

"You will stay here as long as we want you," Varkov said. "My men can find the manuscript, as long as you tell us everything you know. If you don't, you can forget about seeing your girlfriend again." Varkov turned to the colonel. "I think we're about ready for my people to go to work on him."

Colonel Tarygin's face clouded with thought--or was it displeasure? "Just a moment, Varkov," he finally said, arresting Krakin's sudden panic. "This fellow seems to be reasonably competent at what he does. Not as efficient as your men, of course-- it's obvious he lacks the hardness to qualify for your organization. But in this case perhaps we need a man who can achieve a, shall we say, rapport with the possible suspects. I'm sure you understand. We appreciate your efforts in finding Krakin and bringing him to us, although I wish we'd been better informed about the time pressures."

Varkov stood up stiffly. He could tell when he was being dismissed. "Very well, Colonel," he said. "You apparently don't need me any more. I have other jobs." He turned without any further words and went to the door. At a nod from the colonel, the sergeant opened it for him and closed it after Varkov went out.

"Sorry to subject you to that, Krakin, but you brought it on yourself, you know. And don't think you're free of them, either. I can't keep protecting you if you don't produce."

"What's going on, anyway? Why did you bring me out here? What do the Army and the KGB have to do with this?"

"Easy now, Krakin. Let's not ask too many questions. This is an Army project, the whole complex. The KGB handles our security. We didn't want it that way, but even the Army doesn't always get what it wants. Naturally, when you had someone look into the KGB's files for you, they took a personal interest in you."

"But what does this project have to do with me, or with Polokov?"

The Colonel smiled. "For an answer to that question, I'm going to take you to see someone else."

23

Krakin followed Colonel Tarygin out of the interrogation room and down the long white corridor that ran the length of the building. The odors of the building were stronger here, and Krakin concluded they were more like the chemical smell of a laboratory than the antiseptic smell of a hospital.

At the end of the corridor the colonel opened a door into a small reception area. "Is the director in?" he asked a short, thick woman in a white laboratory coat who sat behind a typewriter.

The woman stood up sharply as the colonel addressed her. "Yes, sir. Shall I tell him you're here?"

"Please sit down. We'll just go right on in."

The colonel knocked twice on another door and then opened it. He and Krakin walked into a large office, fully ten meters square. The room was expensively but somewhat dully decorated. It looked to Krakin like Peter Solin's office might look if he was forced to furnish it with domestic products. Behind a desk in one corner of the room, almost buried behind messy stacks of paper and books, sat an intense-looking man of about sixty. He had a broad forehead, wide-set eyes, and a wide mouth. His dark hair made him appear, at first glance, to be younger than he was.

"Denisovich," the colonel said, "I hope you don't mind my interrupting you, but there's someone here I'd like you to meet."

"I don't suppose it would make any difference if I did mind, would it, Colonel," the man said, but with a smile. He rose and approached them. The man carried himself with a great deal of authority, and there was an intelligence in his eyes that was not typical of a high-level bureaucrat. "I'm the director of this project, yet I must get the Colonel's permission before I'm allowed to visit my own laboratories," he said to Krakin, shaking his head. "I guess I'm just not used to being involved with the Army."

"Leo Krakin," the colonel said, "I'd like you to meet Comrade T. D. Lysenko, President of the Lenin Academy of Agricultural Science, Director of the Institute of Genetics of the U.S.S.R. Academy of Sciences, Hero of Socialist Labor, and, as he has already told you, the director of our project."

As Krakin's jaw dropped open in surprise, the colonel spoke to Lysenko. "Krakin is the fellow that Polokov has hired to find his manuscript. Varkov found out about Krakin when Krakin tried to get some information about Polokov from the KGB's own files." At this the colonel shook his head. "So Varkov had him brought here. Comrade Krakin thinks he may still be able to find the manuscript, but he doesn't have much time, because the publishers are scheduled to leave the country on Sunday night."

Lysenko reached out and shook hands with Krakin. "Pleased to meet you, Comrade Krakin," he said. "I imagine you never expected to get into anything like this, did you?" The man was smooth. Very smooth. Not your typical biologist by any means. The contrast with Polokov was startling.

"I still don't quite know what I've got into, Comrade Lysenko." Krakin glanced at the colonel.

"Krakin considers you one of his key suspects for having taken the manuscript. Polokov told him you might have stolen the manuscript because it challenges your theories."

Lysenko laughed. Krakin decided to cross the man off his list of suspects, but not because he wasn't capable of a theft or two to enhance his reputation. He simply did not appear to have anything to fear from Polokov.

"That's really very funny, Krakin. Your Polokov has an awfully high regard for himself. Of course, I don't agree with

Polokov's ideas. He's wrong, and it would be a waste of ink and paper for his precious manuscript to be published in this country. But I hardly have to steal it to prevent that from happening." Lysenko and the colonel exchanged smiles. "Now if Polokov has in mind publishing in some Western country--and that, I assume, is his intention, is it not?" Krakin nodded. "Then I couldn't care less. He can only take the West further into the dead end of Mendelism, and that is no concern of mine. The West has already been so stupid as to reject my theories. Their heads are in the clouds, Krakin, the biologists of the West. Here our theories are based upon practice, upon what we actually see happening in the fields." Lysenko's tone had become almost pedantic.

"If all this is so," Krakin asked, "why did you bring me here?"

"We didn't bring you," the colonel said. "Varkov and his men did. And that was largely your own fault."

"As far as we're concerned," Lysenko added, "you can go back and do anything you wish for Polokov. I just hope he pays you well."

"Thank you." Krakin looked from Lysenko to the colonel, then back to Lysenko. "Before I go, might I ask what this project, whatever it is, has to do with Polokov, or with me? The answer could help me find the manuscript."

Lysenko looked questioningly at the colonel, who nodded. "Please sit down," Lysenko said to Krakin. Krakin sat in a plastic chair near Lysenko's desk. Lysenko began to pace slowly back and forth across the room. The colonel remained standing where he was.

"This project," Lysenko said, "is, as you might have guessed, very secret. So, naturally, I can't tell you everything about it. But I believe I can answer your question.

"What we're doing here involves agricultural development. Producing new strains of plants, and so forth. This kind of work requires application of the theories I've spent my life developing. Naturally, we're highly interested in the work of others in the same field. If they have sound ideas, we want to take advantage of them. But if they have unsound ideas, we don't want to be contaminated and misled by them. Consequently we are constantly screening the work of men like Polokov."

"But his theories aren't helpful to you."

"Correct. In fact, they are detrimental. They could only undermine our work." Lysenko stopped his pacing in front of Krakin. "Tell me, Krakin, what do you know of Polokov's theories?"

"Only a little. Just what he told me, and that wasn't much."

"Well, his basic point is that an organism's characteristics are determined entirely by the inherited genetic makeup of its parents. Like the Western biologists, he believes that an acquired characteristic cannot be transmitted to a future generation. He also believes that the extent to which an environment can influence an organism's development is very small. Do you follow that?"

"I think so."

"Well, it's all so much garbage. It is idealistic and it is contrary to the teachings of Darwin. In my experiments, Krakin, I've taken two seeds from the same plant, and by varying the soil conditions and the nutrients, made one grow much larger and more productive plant than the other. And furthermore, when seeds from these two plants are taken and grown under identical conditions, the seeds from the larger plant *continue* to produce larger plants. What do you think of that, Krakin?"

Krakin shrugged his shoulders. "I'm a journalist, not a scientist."

"Well, you've still got a brain. Use it! Why, according to Polokov's theory, the only way organisms will ever change is by spontaneous mutation. To a scientist, Comrade Krakin, that's no explanation at all. It's like saying the reason the sun comes up in the morning is because it does. Spontaneous mutation, indeed! One might as well attribute changes in organisms to God."

Krakin watched the colonel as Lysenko went on with the lecture. He stood impassively, taking it all in. There was something odd here. This was a show being put on for Krakin's benefit, though who was responsible for it was not entirely clear. Lysenko seemed genuine enough--and perhaps not so different from Polokov as Krakin had first thought, despite their scientific disagreement.

"So you see, Krakin," Lysenko concluded, returning to his desk, "we would not want Polokov's manuscript published in our country. That explains our concern. But we have no objection to its being published elsewhere. The West deserves Polokov."

"So, Krakin," added Colonel Tarygin, "we would like for you to find this manuscript. It would be helpful to us to know where it is."

"Obviously *we* don't have it," Lysenko said, laughing again.

The three of them were silent for a moment. Finally, Krakin spoke. "Well, I take it that I may go now? I'll have to hurry to get back to Basilgrad in time to do anything. The train took well over a day to get me here from Leningrad."

The colonel looked at Lysenko thoughtfully. "Perhaps, Denisovich," he said, "we should arrange more rapid transportation for Comrade Krakin."

"Can you do it?" Lysenko asked.

"Yes. We'll put him on a transport plane this afternoon. I'll make the arrangements."

Lysenko stepped up to Krakin, who rose from his chair. "Very good to see you, Comrade Krakin. Good luck to you." They shook hands again and Lysenko went back to his desk and resumed his work, ignoring Krakin and the colonel.

The colonel put his hand on Krakin's shoulder and ushered him to the door. "Comrade Krakin, we're sorry for the inconvenience of bringing you here, but we have obtained some useful information. You can go on with your job now without further interference from us. As long, of course, as you don't make any more wrong moves."

They were out in the corridor now, walking back toward the building entrance. Krakin's fears had subsided, with one small reservation. What the hell did the colonel consider a "wrong move?"

24

The sleek silver TU-l04 touched down at the Basilgrad Airport and taxied to a stop just off the main runway, a good half a kilometer away from the terminal building. They had raced the sun from Sverdlovsk and lost, but not by much. There was still a residue of gray in the western sky as Krakin jumped down from the plane, followed by two sergeants in dress uniform. They had put him on the plane at Sverdlovsk and sat with him in silence the whole trip, not showing any curiosity as to why such an undistinguished civilian merited the huge transport all to himself.

Krakin, of course, had a thing or two to puzzle out. A few answers he thought he had figured, but most of the questions stubbornly remained.

The sergeants escorted Krakin across the empty runways to one of the gates of the civilian terminal building. There was no shelter from the biting wind out there in the open, and it cut through them like a knife. Once inside the terminal, Krakin put down his suitcase and rubbed his hands together and stamped his feet to restore the circulation. The sergeants nodded to him and then left together, headed back to the plane. Krakin watched as they jogged across the tarmac. Once they were on board, the plane's engines whined louder and it moved slowly back out to the end of the runway, apparently to return to Sverdlovsk without even a pause to refuel.

Krakin walked along the dimly lit corridor until he came to the main waiting area at the center of the terminal. He stopped and looked around. There were no security agents to check his papers, no customs officers, not even any airport clerks to record his arrival. Either he was unexpected, or his way had been cleared. A few maintenance workers were going about their chores on the other side of the waiting area. And off to his left a group of passengers--mostly fat, balding men in gray suits, wearing the sanctimonious expressions of middle-level party bureaucrats--was coming out the door of what appeared to be a V.I.P. meeting room.

Otherwise the terminal was silent. Where else in the world, Krakin wondered, was there a modern airport like this that stood virtually deserted at 6:00 p.m. on a Friday afternoon?

A broad-shouldered man detached himself from the group of bureaucrats and moved toward Krakin. One look at his scarred face told Krakin all he needed to know. Security. Was he already back in trouble again?

"Would you please identify yourself?" the man asked.

"My name is Krakin. Leo Krakin."

"Let me see your papers."

Krakin handed them over. The man looked through them quickly.

"You have no travel authorizations here. No tickets. What are you doing here?"

"I just got off a plane."

"Impossible. There have been no flights scheduled into this airport for an hour. I put the last incoming group on the bus myself. Perhaps you'd better come with me."

Krakin cringed. Suddenly, he thought: why the hell am I letting this guy do this to me? For once, he had the upper hand.

"Don't try to order me around, or I'll have your ass."

The security man stood stock still and blinked. He was definitely not accustomed to such remarks being directed at him.

"Perhaps you'd better explain yourself," he finally said. His tone was half deferential, half belligerent. He obviously couldn't make up his mind. Krakin had him.

"Colonel Tarygin just flew me in here from Sverdlovsk for a special assignment. If you didn't have so much hair in your ears, you'd have heard the plane taking off to go back there a minute ago. Now leave me alone."

The man stayed next to Krakin. He still looked confused. "You're not KGB," he finally said.

"You're damn right. The colonel put me on this job because the KGB can't handle it." Krakin was enjoying this. A few of the bureaucrats heading for the departure gate were casting glances in their direction. "Now, you can call the control tower and check me out if you want, but if you delay me ten more seconds I'll have you on permanent sentry duty in the Arctic Circle."

The man backed away a step. Krakin reached out and retrieved his papers from the man's hand and started to walk away, then turned. "Oh, by the way, you're to forget you ever saw me here. Understand?" The man nodded slowly, and Krakin continued on. Halfway across the waiting area, Krakin glanced back to see him talking furiously on a building telephone and looking Krakin's way. Krakin gave the man a little wave, then went on out of the terminal building. No one followed him.

The buses were all gone, but Krakin managed to wake a taxi driver who was dozing in a little shack next to where the airport's half dozen cabs were parked. After more than a little arguing and cajoling, Krakin got the driver to agree to take him into the city. He almost had to ask the driver to go check with the security guard as to whether Krakin was authorized to use a cab, but finally managed to win his point without that.

25

The taxi dropped Krakin in front of his apartment building. He paid the driver, wondering how he could justify the expense to his editor. Perhaps he would be wiser to say nothing. He still had an unused Leningrad to Basilgrad rail ticket, which he ought to be able to sell to Peter Solin.

Krakin went up to his apartment. Oddly, the door was slightly open and lights were on inside. Krakin stopped in front of the door and stood there silently. What should he do now? He ached to be inside his own retreat. But who was waiting for him in there?

Then he heard the soft humming from inside. He smiled to himself. It was Anya. That was even better than getting home. He pushed the door wide open.

"Hello, Krakin. Nice to see you again." The voice came from the chair just inside the door. It wasn't Anya's. Krakin looked into Andrews' handsome, tanned face.

Anya poked her head out of the kitchen. "Is that you, Leo?" Seeing that it was, she rushed up to him and embraced him. "I've been so worried about you."

"What's he doing here?" Krakin asked, pointing toward Andrews.

"He was waiting for you when I got here. I sort of expected you to be on tonight's train, so I came over to meet you. He says he's a friend of yours from Leningrad. He is, isn't he?"

"In a way."

Anya looked relieved. "He said he was afraid you were tied up and might not have made the train this morning, but he decided to wait and see." She frowned. "The train must have been early. It's only seven o'clock."

"Trains in this country are *never* early," Andrews said. "Therefore, you didn't come by train. Not today's train, anyway. Right, Krakin?"

"What do you want, anyway?" Krakin was irritated at Andrews' presence and didn't try to conceal it.

"I'm very interested in what you've been doing for the last two days. I've found out who you went with. If you will recall, you possess some information that could prove embarrassing to me."

"Don't worry, Andrews, I haven't given you away. I don't happen to feel like talking to you now, so why don't you leave us your number and I'll call you later."

"Look, this is no joking matter. I've got a lot at stake."

Krakin thought about the big gun undoubtedly concealed under Andrews' coat. "I told you, you don't have anything to worry about. If you want to talk, come see me at my office tomorrow. I'll pretend I'm interviewing you."

Andrews' hand moved slowly across the front of his coat. Krakin tensed. Then Andrews put his hands down and pushed himself out of the chair. "All right," he said. "You're tired after a long trip. I'll see you tomorrow." He went to the door. "I hope, though, that you're not planning on leaving your apartment tonight."

"Don't worry. I'll be right here."

"All right. Nice to meet you, Miss Malchev," Andrews said to Anya, and he left. Krakin closed the door and locked it.

Krakin looked at Anya. "I'd advise you to stay here with me tonight."

"Is that why you wouldn't talk to him? To have an excuse to make me stay?"

"Only partly. There's another minor reason. Once I tell him what he wants to know, he might just kill me. You, too, if you're handy."

"Leo, I don't like your jokes."

"No joke. A little far-fetched, maybe, but no joke."

"You're going to tell me about it, aren't you?"

"In the kitchen. God knows where he might have planted his bugs." They went into the kitchen and Krakin swung the door shut. He put his noisiest kettle on to boil. Then he poured two tumblers of vodka, and they sat down at the little table. Krakin started with his arrival in Leningrad on Wednesday evening. He finished with his arrival back in Basilgrad this evening, and the tumblers were empty. As Krakin refilled them, he laughed about the security man at the airport.

"So that's it," Krakin said. "What do you make of it?"

"Why would Andrews want to kill you? He doesn't seem to have anything to do with the manuscript."

"Well, I said it was a little far-fetched. But I'm the only witness to his killing Tvori."

"He did that to protect you. That's not a crime."

Krakin thought for a moment. "Perhaps you're right," he said.

He waved his hand, a bit clumsily. "I don't have time to worry about him. What do you think of the interest the KGB and the Army are taking in me?"

"It scares me. It's partly my fault. I should never have called Karin. You must have been frightened."

"A little."

"Thank goodness that colonel was there." Anya shuddered a little bit. She took a sip from her glass.

"The question, though, is why was he there? Not to help me, that's clear. I've been thinking about this all the way back. I'm sure, Anya, that Colonel Tarygin wants me to find that manuscript and sell it to Putney for Polokov."

"Why?"

"I don't know. I have some guesses, but I really don't know."

"It's got something to do with that factory or whatever you call it out in Sverdlovsk, doesn't it, Leo?"

"I'm sure it does."

"What are they making there?"

"I don't know that either. It smelled like a hospital, or a chemical factory."

"But Lysenko isn't a chemist. He's a biologist."

"He told me they were doing experimental plant breeding. Maybe that's all it is."

"In a place like that?"

"The agriculture five-year plan is six years behind."

"But why is the Army in charge?"

"I don't know. I just don't know." Krakin drank again and they sat in silence for a few minutes, looking into each other's eyes.

Anya reached out and Krakin took her hand. "Leo," she said in a quiet voice, "what if you don't find the manuscript?"

Krakin shrugged.

"The Army will give you back to the KGB, won't it?"

"Possibly. But not necessarily."

"Oh, Leo, what are you going to do?"

"I'm going to find the manuscript and sell it to Putney."

"But where?"

"I have some ideas. And I'll start on them first thing in the morning. Until then, I'm going to concentrate on you and that dinner we're going to cook. The condemned man gets a last wish with his last meal, you know."

26

The next morning, Saturday, Krakin and Anya walked together from Krakin's apartment to the tram stop. The skies were heavy and it felt a little warmer. It looked like it was going to snow. Anya's car came first, and she waved Krakin good-bye. The Central Square tram came a few minutes later. Krakin got on and went to the back, where he could watch out the rear window. The little gray Moskvitch that had been parked a block away pulled out after the tram, leaving small clouds of exhaust hanging in the cold, moist air. It was virtually impossible to follow anyone inconspicuously by automobile in this city, where the trucks, trains and buses outnumbered the private cars ten to one. So Andrews wasn't even trying. Maybe he didn't even want to be inconspicuous.

Sulka was already in when Krakin arrived at his office. The editor hustled over to Krakin's desk.

"You're back," Sulka said.

"Did you think I might not be?"

"One never knows. The KGB was asking about you."

"I know."

"Well, do you have it?"

Krakin tensed. "Have what?"

"The article. On the interviews with the Western publishers."

Krakin relaxed. "I've decided," Sulka continued, "that I'd like to print it as soon as possible. We're getting pressure from the Central

Committee for more ideology."

"Ivan, I didn't realize you wanted it so soon. I've got pages of notes, but I don't have it written in final form. How would Monday be?" Krakin wondered to himself where he had put his outline. He'd almost forgotten the article.

Sulka looked upset. "What have you been doing for three days anyhow?"

"You'd be surprised. Look, Ivan, I've got my outline all finished. I can have the article by Monday afternoon."

"Well, get to work on it."

"Here?" Krakin was baffled by Sulka's odd behavior. "You know I don't work well here."

"I don't care where you work. Just get it written, and as soon as possible." Sulka cast a quick glance back toward his office.

Was Sulka trying to tell him something, Krakin wondered. The article wasn't expected today.

"Well, maybe I'll go someplace where I can work on this thing undisturbed," Krakin said.

"Whatever will get it done the soonest."

Krakin got up from his desk. He and Sulka exchanged looks. Krakin couldn't read anything in Sulka's face. He went out of the office. The gray car was parked about half a block away, on the side of the street away from the square. Krakin walked away from it. The car started up and moved slowly after him. Krakin considered walking across the square to the KGB minister's office just to see what would happen but decided that was too risky, for more than one reason. He turned a corner instead and headed away from the square. The car followed. He walked faster and turned again, and again, and now he was heading back toward the square.

Krakin was beginning to perspire under his heavy coat. Andrews' car was still behind him. The hell with it, Krakin thought. He was now back on the corner next to the *Party Organ* building. A few flakes of snow were beginning to fall in the square. A tram was stopping on the other side of the street. Krakin dashed across and got on. He looked out the back window to see if the car was following. It was. But he saw something else, too. Running up to the corner where Krakin had just stood, an exasperated expression on his face, looking after Krakin's tram, was Jan Kirus.

Krakin had not one, but two tails. He wasn't sure that he liked all the attention.

27

The tram stopped at the University and Krakin trudged across the campus to the Biological Sciences Building. The snow was falling a little harder now, melting on the sidewalk but coating the dirty snow already on the ground elsewhere with a layer of white. Krakin couldn't see either Andrews or Kirus, but he knew they were there. They didn't have to think very hard to know where he was going.

The door to Polokov's office was open and Krakin walked right in. Polokov was at his desk, writing. When he saw Krakin he jumped up.

"Krakin. I've been wondering where you were. Have you found it?" Polokov's eyes were bright with expectation.

"Not yet."

Polokov's expression darkened. "But the publisher is in Basilgrad now," he whined. "He leaves tomorrow."

"I'm doing the best I can, Professor. I've got some good leads. Don't give up yet. I need some more information from you."

"What do you want to know?"

"Well, first of all, Professor, can you think of any reason why your friend Comrade Lysenko would *want* your book to be published in the West?"

"No, I can't. Why do you ask such a foolish question?"

"Because Lysenko told me he didn't care if you sold your book to Putney."

"You saw Lysenko? That's impossible."

"I saw him. At a factory near Sverdlovsk."

"What on earth were you doing there?"

"It's a long story, which I'll tell you some other time. The important thing is that Lysenko seems actually to want your book published. That makes me suspicious."

"Oh, no. That's good news."

"But he may be setting you up for an arrest."

Polokov waved his hand, as if brushing the suggestion aside. "He could do that already, if he wanted to."

Krakin rubbed his chin and looked at Polokov. "Tell me, Professor," he said, "is there anything in your book that would be useful to someone doing work on plant breeding?"

"Of course. Not specific technical information, but my book shows the kinds of methods that will work and the kinds that won't. Most of Soviet agricultural experimental work, Krakin, is absolutely a waste of time. They're trying to develop the inheritance of acquired characteristics, which my studies show is impossible."

"Lysenko told me that this factory in Sverdlovsk is for work on plant breeding. Do you know anything about it--the factory?"

"No. But you don't call a plant breeding station a factory. It's more of a farm than anything."

"This was a whole complex of buildings. I didn't see any cultivated land anywhere around it."

"Then it wasn't a plant breeding station. Unless . . ." Polokov paused.

"Unless what?"

"Unless they're trying to grow plants without soil. Hydroponics. Or unless they're growing algae, or fungus, or something like that. But that would be ridiculous. They wouldn't waste Lysenko's time or the State's money on something like that."

That was it. Now it fit together. Polokov had given Krakin the clue that explained the Sverdlovsk project. But it didn't put him any closer to finding the manuscript. He decided to change the subject.

"Where are your two assistants? Kirus and Togorny?"

Polokov looked at his watch. "In classes. They don't come to the lab until the afternoon on Saturdays."

"They don't have any bright new ideas about your manuscript, do they?"

"What do you mean?"

"Never mind."

"They didn't take the manuscript, Krakin."

"You know, for some reason I think you're right." It seemed fairly clear that Polokov hadn't asked Kirus to follow Krakin. Kirus was doing it on orders from someone else.

"Krakin, I thought you were going to Leningrad to see Putney."

"I did. He couldn't tell me any more than you did. I also found Tvori. I wasn't able to ask him anything, but I did search his apartment. He didn't have the manuscript."

Polokov was agitated. "Well, Krakin, what are you going to do? You don't seem to have any leads at all. Lysenko doesn't have it. Kirus and Togorny don't have it. Tvori doesn't have it. Who does have it? You don't still suspect my wife?"

"No."

"Then where do you think the manuscript is? *I* certainly don't have it. Putney leaves tomorrow evening. You've got to find it." Polokov's tone alternated between a demand and a plea.

"Has Putney been in touch with you since he arrived in Basilgrad?"

"No. I'm supposed to call him at his hotel."

"Then you haven't heard from him since Tvori contacted you several weeks ago."

"That's right."

"Do you know for sure that he's here?"

"The *Red Banner* yesterday said the publishers were scheduled to arrive. Surely he must be with them. Premier Khrushchev is going to be in Basilgrad later today to greet them, according to the newspaper."

"Khrushchev? Here? I didn't know about that."

"Here, read it yourself." Polokov dug around on his desk until he found the newspaper. He handed it to Krakin, who scanned it quickly. Polokov had told him everything of significance.

"This may create some problems in reaching Putney. There will be very heavy security while the Premier is here. What hotel did he say he would be staying at?"

"The Cosmopolitan. Are you going to go see him before you've even found the book?"

"Perhaps, but there are some other things I've got to do first." Krakin moved to the door.

"*Please* help me, Krakin."

"I'll do what I can."

Krakin jerked the door open quickly. An ear was moving away from it, but not fast enough.

"Hear anything interesting, Kirus?" Krakin asked.

"I don't know what you're talking about. I was just coming to see the professor."

"You shouldn't be cutting classes, Kirus. The Party would disapprove." Krakin brushed past the student, giving him an unobtrusive shoulder in the general vicinity of the collarbone. Kirus winced and stepped back but didn't retaliate. Krakin walked briskly down the stairs and out of the building.

28

The snow had stopped momentarily but it threatened to return. Krakin went back to the boulevard and, after a short wait, boarded a tram for the riverfront. Not until he was halfway there did he spot the gray car behind him. It gave him a certain comfort. He was afraid Andrews had gotten lost.

There was still activity in the market below the highway,

although the farmers in most of the stalls were packing up their wagons. Krakin went directly to Solin's building. Fortunately, he was in. The old girl announced Krakin's arrival and showed him into Solin's office. Solin was talking on the telephone. He motioned Krakin to sit down. Krakin did.

Solin was speaking into an ornate, gold-plated instrument of obvious Western manufacture. "How many?" he was asking. "Where?" He paused. "You're sure about the source?" Pause. "All right. Don't do anything unless I tell you. Good job, Josef." He hung up.

Solin looked up at Krakin. "Why do you come here, Krakin?" he said sharply. "You know I can't help you. You're bringing me trouble."

"You live with trouble, Peter. You can handle it. All I want is to ask you about one thing. What do you know about Laszlo Tvori?"

"You mean the late Laszlo Tvori? Did you kill him, Krakin? I didn't know that sort of thing was included in your line of business."

"You mean he's dead?"

Solin laughed at this, but when he spoke again his voice was not friendly. "I don't know what game you're playing, Krakin, but I don't want any part of it. I should have thrown you out the first time you came."

"What have I done to threaten you?"

"It's the company you keep. You're way over your head, Krakin. You're way over *my* head. Now get out of here. I don't want your friends out there involved in my business."

"You mean Andrews? He's just a news correspondent. What can he do to you?"

"My friend Krakin, at this moment there are at least five people watching for you to leave this building. The correspondent, as you call him, is described by my people as a high level American intelligence agent. There are two students out there, a man and a woman, who are definitely known to be in the employ of the Soviet Army High Command. And there are two gorillas at the corner who must be KGB agents; they sure as hell aren't cabbage farmers."

"The KGB? They're watching me too?"

"Draw your own conclusions. Now please leave before they come after you. If they do, I'm going to turn you over to them."

"All right. But please, just answer my question. Do you know something about Lazslo Tvori?"

"A completely untrustworthy small-time errand boy. My people would never have used him. He was mixed up in espionage, which made him totally useless. Furthermore, he was inclined to try to work for several employers at once on the same matter--without their knowledge, of course."

"That's it?"

"That's it. I've found out nothing about your precious manuscript and I've stopped trying. Now please leave."

"Thank you for your hospitality, Peter. You're a real gentleman. You may have helped me more than you realize."

29

Krakin went down to the ground floor of Solin's building and peeked cautiously out the door. He couldn't see Andrews' car or either of Polokov's assistants, but he did spot the two heavy-set men on the corner. They were KGB, all right. Apparently Varkov hadn't entirely given up, after all. They would be especially interested in him after a visit to Solin. Krakin stayed inside the building and considered. Why not just check to see if there was a back door to this place?

Krakin went to the back of the building and poked around. No door. Only an old metal stairway spotted with rust. Then Krakin thought about the rising grade from the river. He ascended the steps and went through an opening onto the next floor. There was the door. He tried the handle. It wouldn't turn. Locked? He inspected it. It too was old and rusty. He tried it again. Slowly it turned, and then the door opened toward him on squeaky hinges. He looked out. A passageway with steep brick walls at the sides led away from the building. He could see the sky above the passageway but not much light penetrated into it. Well, it was better than facing the KGB agents. He went out, closed the door behind him, and started down the passageway.

"Okay, Krakin, don't move." The voice boomed down at Krakin from above and echoed hollowly in the narrow passageway. Krakin looked up. A man's head and shoulders were silhouetted against the sky. His features were in shadow but Krakin had no trouble recognizing Andrews' voice. Nor did he have any doubt as to what Andrews was holding in his hand, pointed at Krakin's chest.

"I had a hunch you might try to slip away through the back door. Especially when I saw those other guys. KGB, don't you think?"

"What do you want?"

"I want to talk with you. I've been polite. I came to see you at your apartment, and you threw me out. I was going to see you at your office, as you suggested, and you left before I had a chance. I'm not going to wait any more. Especially with the KGB on your tail. If they grab you again, I may not have another opportunity. Who knows what fabrications you may tell them about me."

As Andrews talked, Krakin searched for an escape route. The only way was back into the building, and Andrews could empty his gun into Krakin before Krakin could get that door open again. Andrews might not shoot, but at the moment Krakin didn't feel like taking the chance.

"All right. Where do you want to talk?"

"My car. Come on out of there."

Krakin went to the end of the passageway and climbed a set of crumbling concrete stairs. They led to a tiny, snow-covered yard. Andrews, his gun still out, moved next to Krakin. He pointed toward a brick wall at the back of the yard. "There's an alleyway on the other side of that wall," he said. "That's where my car is."

"You can put the gun away. I'll come with you. It makes me nervous."

Andrews looked at Krakin for a moment, then unbuttoned his coat and slid the gun into its holster under his left arm. The two men went together through a rusty iron gate and into the alley. They got in Andrews' car and drove through the alley to one of the streets leading down to the riverfront drive. Andrews turned right, away from the river. They proceeded on for several minutes in silence, Andrews glancing continually at the rear view mirror. Then he turned left, along a road paralleling the river.

"Are they following us?" Krakin asked.

"I don't think so."

"Where are we going? I thought you wanted to talk in the car."

"A place that's safe."

The car sped on, toward the Central Square. Andrews turned right as he approached the square and then left again, around it. About one kilometer beyond the square they entered the part of Basilgrad that had been informally set aside for foreign residents. They passed apartment buildings and consulates. Suddenly they slowed in front of one of the latter, a huge, white pre-revolution mansion surrounded by a high wrought iron fence. Andrews turned sharply through the open gate. Krakin, glancing out the back window, noticed three uniformed men closing it. The car crunched up the long gravel drive, around to the back of the building, and then down an incline into an underground garage. Krakin was in foreign territory.

30

Andrews parked the car, got out, and came around and opened Krakin's door. "Come on." He grabbed Krakin's arm and led him up a flight of stairs and into a large hallway, paneled in dark wood. No one else was around. Andrews waited for a moment, listening, and then took Krakin to a small library. It was a comfortable room, with books lining the walls, a large table and chairs in the center, and leather upholstered armchairs. Through leaded casement windows Krakin could see the snow beginning again, falling softly on the grounds outside the building.

"Nice place," Krakin said. "Is it yours?"

"Don't be funny, Krakin. Sit down."

They both sat, Krakin in one of the leather armchairs, Andrews at one of the straight-backed chairs at the table. Andrews surveyed Krakin's face for a moment before he spoke. "This is my country's unofficial consulate. I didn't have to bring you here, but I did. It's a risk, of course, but I believe I understand you well enough to make it worth taking."

"Is that what you wanted to talk to me about?"

"Goddamn it, Krakin, cut out that shit, will you?" Andrews stood and glared down at Krakin. "This is a serious matter."

"I sort of gathered that from the fact that you brought me here at gunpoint."

"You wise-ass son of a bitch." Andrews stepped toward Krakin, drew back his fist, and started a backhand blow at Krakin's face. Instantly Krakin grabbed the swinging arm and used its momentum to pull Andrews forward. He rose out of his chair and brought the arm up sharply behind Andrews' back. He slammed Andrews forward into a shelf of books, pinning his shoulder holster down and denying Andrews access to his gun.

"I may look like some dumb peasant," Krakin said with clenched teeth, "but I'm not. I don't like being pushed around, by you or anyone else."

"All right. All right. I'm sorry. I'm on your side, believe me. The gun just seemed the only way to get your attention." Then, in a louder voice, Andrews called, "Okay. I'm all right. Leave us alone."

Krakin glanced behind him and saw two guards, in American military uniforms, look at each other questioningly and then slowly back out of the room. Krakin hadn't even heard them come in. He released Andrews' arm.

Andrews rubbed the arm, then brushed his wrinkled jacket,

straightened his tie, pushed his mussed hair back into place and, watching Krakin carefully, walked around him and back to the chair at the library table. Krakin sat down again also.

"The first thing I'd like to know is what happened to you after I left you in Leningrad."

Krakin hesitated. He had thought that he didn't care who knew about the Sverdlovsk factory. Now he wasn't so sure. "The KGB came and got me. I thought you knew that."

"Why?"

"They wanted to know about my interest in Polokov."

"But why? Why the KGB? You're not in their league."

"I've already been told that once today. I had tried to get some information from their files. They didn't seem to care for that."

"Jesus Christ, was that dumb! You're lucky you're still alive. What were you looking for?"

"Just their file on Polokov."

Andrews' eyes narrowed. "What made you think they had a file on Polokov?"

"They have a file on everybody, don't they?"

"Don't give me that crap. Why did you think they had a file on Polokov?"

Krakin shrugged. "Polokov thought the KGB might have taken his manuscript. I wanted to find out if this was a real possibility. If the KGB had anything to do with it, I didn't want to touch it."

"At least that was sensible. Where did the KGB take you?"

"I don't know. They put me on a train without any windows and took me some place and asked me questions."

"Then what?"

"They brought me back to Basilgrad."

"And shook your hand and apologized for the inconvenience?"

"Not exactly."

"Bullshit, Krakin. I don't believe a word of it. I know something about the KGB. If you tried to get something from their files and they knew about it they would never release you so easily."

"Maybe they figure I'm too valuable to my magazine."

"What did you tell them about me?"

"They already knew that I'd talked with you. I didn't tell them anything else."

"What about Tvori?"

"They asked about him, but I didn't get around to telling them he's dead, and that's one thing they didn't seem to already know."

"Did you tell them you went to see Tvori?"

"Yes."

"And that I was with you?"

"Yes."

"What else?"

"That's about it."

"What do you mean, that's about it?"

"That's all I said. Then they changed the subject. I didn't have to decide whether to tell them what you did."

Andrews got up and walked to the window and looked out at the snow. "You know, Krakin, that's about the most unbelievable story I've ever heard. And I've heard a lot of them in my business."

Krakin wanted to ask what business Andrews was referring to, but he refrained. "Well, it's true. The KGB hasn't come after you, has it?"

"Not yet." Andrews looked back toward Krakin. "Maybe they're waiting until after the publishers leave."

"Then you'll know tomorrow."

"Tonight. The publishers are leaving tonight." Andrews looked at his watch. "In about four hours. The Premier is giving them a big reception at the airport starting in a few minutes."

Krakin swallowed hard. He felt the sudden, sinking feeling of imminent failure. "But they were scheduled to go tomorrow."

"Some of the publishers insisted on going early. They made a big stink, so the government moved up the schedule. Canceled the compulsory sightseeing for tomorrow. The reception with Kruschchev was scheduled for tonight anyway."

Krakin tried hard to think, but he had difficulty concentrating. "These publishers who insisted on leaving early. They didn't include

Putney, by any chance?"

"As a matter of fact, he was one of the instigators. Apparently that doesn't surprise you."

"No, it doesn't. It tends to confirm what I already thought. About the manuscript."

"The manuscript? Oh, forget about that. There's nothing you can do."

Krakin got up. "That's the whole reason I'm here. Look, Andrews, I can't play your game any more. I've got things to do and I don't have much time."

Andrews' frowned. "I'm afraid not, Krakin. I can't let you go."

"Look, I've told you everything I know," Krakin shot back angrily. "Now let me out of here."

"I'm not finished with my questions, Krakin, but even if I were I can't let you leave. You may not have told the KGB anything yet, but as long as you're alive and roaming around this city, they'll get it from you someday. Whether you want them to or not."

"You mean you're going to give me the same as Tvori?" Krakin asked the question lightly, but it was, he realized, not a frivolous question.

"If necessary, yes. In your case, however, I think I can offer an alternative that will be more pleasant for you and considerably easier for me to explain."

"What are you talking about?"

"Very simple, Mr. Krakin. You're going to defect."

31

"You're crazy," Krakin said.

Andrews shook his head. "No way. It's the perfect solution to our little problem. You're not cut out for this socialist society, Krakin.

You're a free spirit. You'll love America. And as for me, I'll be off the spot. You won't be available to the KGB any more to tell them about Tvori, and I can explain my meetings with you in case anyone asks me."

"There are people here I don't want to leave."

"You mean Miss Malchev? Don't worry. She can come along with you. I've already got people working on the papers."

"What's the catch?"

"Catch? No catch. You're doing me a favor, and I'm doing you one. Of course, you'll be expected to undergo questioning, just to see if you have any helpful information. It's the least you can do to repay us for getting you out of here. There needn't be any fear of reprisal from your old comrades here. After all, you'll be in the United States, where human rights mean something."

Krakin didn't say anything for a minute. He had never seriously considered the possibility of leaving the U.S.S.R.

"What happens if I refuse?" Krakin asked.

Andrews spread his hands apart and then patted his coat under his left shoulder. "I really wouldn't have any alternative."

"I've been wondering about something, Andrews. Was that shot back in Leningrad meant for Tvori or for me?"

Andrews gave a smirk of confidence. "I don't miss what I aim at, Krakin."

"That gives me a little comfort."

"Not much. It was a hard decision."

Krakin stared at Andrews' face, the even teeth spreading again into a broad grin. Now *he* had to make a hard decision. Perhaps the most important of his life. He had the feeling that somehow this was where events had been taking him ever since he first set foot inside Polokov's office. Or maybe since long before that. He thought about defection. No more KGB. No more plans to fulfill. No more travel permits or internal passports. He could live where he wished, work at what he wished, write and speak as he wished, and earn whatever his talents were worth. And here it was, all laid out on a silver platter. He would be a fool—an utter fool—to pass up an opportunity like this.

But he said, "I can't do it. I haven't recovered the manuscript for Polokov."

Andrews began to laugh, then stopped. "Don't tell me you really mean that. Look, Krakin, that manuscript is insignificant--it's nothing--compared to what I'm offering you. You don't owe Polokov anything." He paused, then went on. "Besides, I think you know where the manuscript is."

"I do."

"Then you also know that I can't let you get it."

"I don't really want the manuscript now. I just want the money for it."

Andrews shook his head. "I'm afraid not."

"Then I can't defect." The decision was really inevitable, Krakin realized. And it wasn't because of any obligation to Polokov. Krakin was no fan of socialism, but he was no fan of capitalism either. Abstract ideology meant little to him. He could eat, sleep, work, play, love, and enjoy music, art, theater, literature, sports and the company of friends just as well in a socialist world as a capitalist one. The terror that once ruled the U.S.S. R. had dissipated enough to be joked about, whereas by all reports crime was increasingly rampant in the West. Most importantly, what good were his talents, honed to a fine edge through years of struggle with the Socialist machine, where there was no such machine?

"I can't defect," Krakin repeated. "You'll have to let me go. I've got a lot to do tonight." As soon as the words were spoken Krakin began to reconsider. Perhaps his request wasn't exactly correct. A plan was taking shape in his mind.

"Apparently you didn't understand me." Andrews now sounded a bit annoyed. "You don't have a choice. If you won't defect, I'll have to kill you. I don't want to do that. I rather like you, Krakin."

"I've changed my mind. "

"That's sensible."

"Yes. Instead of leaving here and finding that manuscript on my own, I'm going to have your help."

"What?" Andrews' mouth opened wide. "I don't like your

jokes, Krakin. They aren't funny. Let's get down to business. I've got a stack of papers for you to sign."

"You can shove your papers up your ass. I'm not joking. I'm not going to defect. You're not going to kill me. You *are* going to help me. Because if you don't go along with me, the KGB is going to have you and they're going to take you apart with an ice pick."

"What the hell are you talking about?"

"After you dropped me at my hotel in Leningrad, and before the KGB picked me up, I took a few precautions. I wrote down everything that happened on hotel stationery and put it in an envelope and mailed it."

"To whom?"

"To myself."

Andrews looked incredulous. "I don't believe it. If you'd mailed it on Wednesday night, it would have arrived by now. And you know damn well the KGB is opening your mail. Hell, they would probably have intercepted it back at the Neva. So why haven't they come after me?"

"Because I put the envelope addressed to me inside another envelope, addressed to another name at a safe place. If I don't pick up the letter by tomorrow night, the inside envelope will be sent to me. And you're right. The KGB will have it within an hour."

"Where did you send the thing?"

"To a place you could never figure out."

"There are ways to make you tell me."

"Maybe. But maybe not. Not in time, anyway. I'm pretty tough."

Andrews rubbed his smooth-shaven cheek thoughtfully for a moment. "Purely as a matter of curiosity, what is it you want me to do?"

"I want you to help me get Polokov's manuscript. Or rather, the money he was promised for it. You have some influence in the appropriate quarters, I'm sure."

"Is that it?"

"That's it."

"You'll destroy the letter?"

"Right."

"I'll have to think about it."

"Think fast, I don't have much time." Krakin got up and started pacing slowly up and down beside the heavy wooden library table. "Oh," he said, "there is one other little thing I'm going to ask that you do."

"What is it?"

"Well, if I destroy the letter, you're still going to worry your head about what I might tell the KGB, so you're still going to want to . . . defect me. Right?"

Andrews didn't say anything.

"Therefore, after you help me get the payment for the manuscript, I'm going to insist that you leave the country. Permanently. I would suggest that you go right along with the Western publishers tonight. Yes, that would be best."

Andrews opened his mouth as if to protest, then closed it. He and Krakin stared at each other for a long moment.

Finally Andrews spoke. "I've never been one to agonize over decisions, Krakin. I've grown a bit tired of this place, anyway. It's very drab, you know, compared to America." He shook his head, looking down. "You've missed a fabulous opportunity to see for yourself." He looked up again at Krakin. "Well, you've got me, Krakin. What is it exactly that you'd like me to do?"

Krakin was surprised at how readily Andrews had conceded. A little too readily, perhaps?

32

Andrews' little gray car sped along the nearly-deserted highway to the Basilgrad airport. The snow was falling in earnest now and the car slid around the road as Andrews maneuvered to avoid the drifts that his headlights illuminated on the road's surface.

"The snow's getting heavier," Krakin said. He was sitting beside Andrews in the front seat of the car. "Maybe they'll delay the flight until tomorrow."

"I doubt it. If anything, the publishers will push to leave earlier."

"They wouldn't just walk out on the Premier."

"Don't bet on it. These guys don't let anything stop them from doing what they want to do. You've figured that out yourself."

They turned onto the airport drive and nearly went off the road. Most of the drive had been plowed, however, and presented no problem. Andrews parked at the curb alongside the terminal building, behind a line of black limousines that awaited the functionaries inside. Krakin and Andrews got out of the car. Andrews stepped to Krakin's side as they moved to the door of the terminal.

"Can I trust you?" Andrews said.

"What?" Krakin looked at Andrews. He was smiling.

"Can I trust you?"

"Like a brother."

"Here." Andrews held out his hand. Krakin took what was in it. The car keys. "Drop them off at the consulate for me, will you?"

"Sure."

They went inside. The waiting area was even more deserted than it had been the day before--was it just the day before?--when Krakin returned from Sverdlovsk. Except around the meeting room that yesterday had been filled with visiting bureaucrats. Tonight dark-suited security men stood virtually shoulder to shoulder around the entrance to the room.

Andrews led Krakin directly up to the security men. "I'm Steven Andrews," he announced to the tall one who stood slightly apart from the others and seemed to be in charge. "I'm an official aide to the publishers. This is my assistant." He pointed to Krakin.

The tall man glanced at Andrews, then looked slowly and deliberately through several sheets of paper on a clipboard he held. "You wait," he said, and he went inside the meeting room.

Krakin didn't like waiting, not in front of all that muscle. He tried hard to look nonchalant and slightly put upon. His gaze drifted from one ugly face to another of the men in front of him, then stopped. There, down near the wall, was the security man with the scarred face who had confronted Krakin at the airport yesterday. And he was staring directly at Krakin, a scowl on his face.

Krakin moved his eyes past the man, pretending not to recognize him. No, that was wrong. The man stirred. Krakin looked at him again, sternly. The man stopped, looking confused. Krakin touched his fingers to his lips in a gesture for silence and continued to glare at him. It seemed to work. The man looked away.

The tall security chief returned from the meeting room, a Westerner following him reluctantly. The Westerner was thin, with plastic-rimmed glasses and long hair. The security chief pointed to Andrews and Krakin.

"Hi, Ralph," Andrews said cheerily.

The Westerner turned to the security man. "Yes. Yes. That's Andrews. Of course he can come in. I don't know the other one, but if he's with Andrews he's okay. Now, will you excuse me." He went back inside.

The security chief nodded to his men in front of the door. They parted ranks and Andrews and Krakin hurried through. As he passed, Krakin glanced again at the man who had recognized him. The man was looking at Krakin. What the hell, Krakin thought. He gave the man a wink, then went through the door.

Inside the room was noisy and smoky. Dumpy women in plain

uniforms carried trays of vodka around. The gathering was impressive. Krakin immediately recognized two members of the Basilgrad Region Central Committee who were talking to each other just inside the door. Other lesser Party lights stood nearby. Oddly, the Russians in the room seemed to outnumber the Westerners.

"I don't see Putney. Do you?" Krakin asked.

Andrews shook his head. He stopped one of the Westerners who was on his way to the other end of the room. "Hi, Tom. Seen Putney?"

Andrews and the man named Tom conversed for a minute out of Krakin's hearing. Tom then pointed in the direction he was heading. Andrews motioned Krakin that they should follow.

As they rounded a corner of the room Krakin could see that there was another door at the back that led out into a corridor--perhaps to the gates to the aircraft. Just in front of the door stood a knot of people. The man named Tom moved into the crowd. Andrews and Krakin did likewise. Both were so intent on keeping up with Tom that neither noticed the short, round man with the balding head who, in the midst of a hearty laugh, was backing away from the center of the group toward them. He bumped into Andrews and careened off into Krakin, almost lost his balance, and then staggered forward. As the round man spun about to see what he had hit, Krakin suddenly felt his arms pinned on either side by two more dark-suited guards, counterparts of the bouncers at the front door. But Krakin didn't pay too much attention to them. He was busy trying to figure out what to say to the short, bald man he had almost knocked over. Krakin had never met Premier Khrushchev before.

Andrews saved him for the moment. "Please excuse us, Mr. Premier," he said. "We were very clumsy."

Khrushchev was frowning. Krakin's arms were beginning to hurt. "Who are you?" the Premier asked Andrews.

"My name is Andrews. I'm the Leningrad correspondent for the International Press. I've been assisting the publishers with their arrangements. This gentleman," he nodded toward Krakin, "is Leo Krakin, who has been helping me."

"Are you in such a hurry to leave that you almost knock me over?"

"Actually, Mr. Premier, I was just going to the men's room." Andrews gave Khrushchev the hearty smile that Krakin had seen before.

The Premier's brow remained furrowed. "And what," Khrushchev said, "was your assistant going to do? Wipe your ass for you?" At this Khrushchev exploded into a huge laugh, his jowls shaking as his head rocked back and forth. The room, which had gone silent at the encounter, became noisy again as the other Party functionaries echoed the Premier's mirth. Krakin happily felt the steel hands that were holding him relax.

Krakin, with all his will power, could not resist the impulse that came over him. "May I take this opportunity," he said, in his best imitation American accent, after the Premier had quieted down, "to compliment you on your understanding and your excellent sense of humor." Khrushchev cocked his head to the side and looked at Krakin quizzically, as if he were hard of hearing. The bodyguards still stood at Krakin's shoulders. The room quieted again.

"You apologize for running into me," Khrushchev said. It was a statement, not a question.

"Of course."

"Then be on your way. And I hope everything comes out all right." The Premier roared again as he turned away from Krakin and back to the Westerners and the Party men he had been talking with. The guards stepped away from Krakin but continued to watch him with cold eyes.

33

Andrews and Krakin waited until Khrushchev became engrossed again in conversation. Then they resumed their search. The man they were following had been waiting for them in the corridor just outside the door.

"Where's Putney?" Andrews asked.

"Not here," the man said. "They were supposed to be here. He must have got on the plane."

"The plane?" Krakin asked. He was growing suspicious.

"Yes," the man said. He looked at Andrews, then at Krakin. "We made arrangements to get the planes to the gate early, so that we can leave right after the reception. We're worried about the snow."

"Where's the plane?" Krakin asked.

"The gate at the end of this corridor. You can't miss it. It's the VIP gate. Just follow me." The man started on down the corridor. Andrews didn't move.

"Come on," Krakin said.

"Just a second, Krakin. You see what's happened? You've passed the security check. They think you're with me. You can get on that plane and when it leaves in an hour or two, you'll be a free man."

"I've made my decision. You're wasting time." They started down the corridor.

"You want to spend the rest of your life in a country run by people like that jackass back there?"

"Watch what you say. You're not out of here yet. You're saying your country isn't run by jackasses?"

Andrews smiled. "Well, at least we elect our jackasses."

"So do we."

"But there's no one else on the ballot."

"Is that so different from having a ballot with two jackasses?"

They had reached the gate. Andrews stopped. "Then you're not coming with us?"

"I'm not. But I'm going on that plane right now to get the money for Polokov's book."

Andrews shrugged. "As you wish." The two of them went out through the glass door and walked under the portable shelter to the steps leading up to the plane. Krakin, without waiting for Andrews, dashed up them. The aircraft was a DC-7 and it bore the markings of a French charter service. Krakin was surprised at the opulence and obvious comfort inside. Soft music came from overhead speakers, and the smell of coffee filled the slightly stale air.

A young woman dressed in a bright uniform and holding a clipboard stood just inside the plane. "Your name?" she asked, poised with a pencil ready to check it off.

Before Krakin could respond, Andrews, who had bounded up the steps right behind him, said, "It's all right, you don't need to check anything. We're just looking around."

The woman smiled sweetly at Andrews. "Anything you say, Mr. Andrews," she said. He took the clipboard from her, looked at it for a moment, made a notation, and handed it back.

Krakin walked on into the plane. They had come in at the rear door, and the plane was empty behind them, so Krakin moved toward the front. His eyes scanned the faces of the passengers as he passed them. A surprising number was already on board the plane. Halfway to the front Krakin still hadn't seen Putney.

"Where is he?" Krakin growled.

"He's here. I'm sure," Andrews said.

Just then the door to the lavatory at the front of the plane opened and closed. A tall, spare frame topped by a bald head emerged and started back down the aisle. It was Putney.

"Putney!" Krakin called.

The bald man looked up. Surprise registered first on his face, followed by furtive glances around the interior of the plane, then a look of resignation. Putney sat down heavily in an empty seat at the front of the cabin, facing away from Krakin. He had not returned

Krakin's greeting.

Krakin walked quickly forward and sat down in the seat next to Putney. They were on the left side of the aisle, Putney next to the window. Andrews followed and stood in the aisle next to Krakin.

"Nice to see you again, Mr. Putney," Krakin said in English.

"What do you want?" Putney was looking out the window at the falling snow.

"I came to see you off. I hope you had a nice stay in Basilgrad."

Putney turned toward Krakin. "I did. It would have been much nicer if you'd located that manuscript for me."

"What makes you think I don't have it?"

"Polokov called and told me. You don't, do you?"

"No."

"That's what I thought. Thank you for seeing me off. You can go now."

"Sure." Krakin started to get up, then sat back down. As he did, he noticed that Andrews had slipped away somewhere. "Oh, I almost forgot. Although I don't have the manuscript, I do know where it is. As a matter of fact, I've come to collect the payment for it."

"I don't know what you're talking about."

"Yes, you do. Mr. Putney, you have the manuscript. You've had it all along. You had Tvori go back and steal it, shortly before Polokov contacted me. That was probably your plan all along. You sent Tvori to make the offer so he could find out where the book was kept. But a deal is a deal. Give me the money."

"That's the craziest thing I've ever heard. What makes you suspect me?"

"Because I've checked out every other possibility and come up with a blank. And because you're a money-grubbing American who would steal from your own mother."

"Listen, you goddamn Communist. Don't talk to me about national moralities. I don't have the damn book. Now get out of here and stop bothering me."

"If that's the way you want to play it, maybe I'll just tell my story to the KGB. They'll search you, of course, and they'll find the book. They may let you leave the country--in about ten years or so. If you survive, that is." Krakin turned away from Putney and started to get out of his seat. He could sense Putney's sudden tenseness behind him.

Just then Andrews appeared again, coming from the front of the plane. "Well," he said, "what's going on?"

"Putney denies having the book stolen. I've no alternative but to tell my story to the KGB. I'm sorry, Andrews, but it looks like you'll be involved, too."

Krakin expected Andrews to see through the bluff, but that didn't matter as long as Putney was hooked. To his great surprise, however, Andrews looked at Putney, spread his hands wide in an expression of resignation, and said, "He's got us. I can't have him going to the KGB. Give him the money."

"What?" Putney looked at Andrews in disbelief.

"Give him the money. He's serious." Andrews turned to Krakin. "Sit down again. We'll work this all out." Krakin, still surprised, slowly sank back into the seat. Putney looked back and forth from Andrews to Krakin. "The money, Putney," Krakin said.

"It's okay. Give it to him," said Andrews.

Putney didn't move. Krakin noticed the cabin lights flicker briefly and heard a dull thud from the back of the plane, but he paid them no attention.

Finally Putney spoke. "Damn you, Andrews, all right. But I'm not paying him anything. He can have the goddamn book back, as long as we get the hell out of here."

Krakin felt a surge of triumph. He was about to accept Putney's offer when he remembered Colonel Tarygin's last words to him. "Don't make any wrong moves," Tarygin had said. Was recovering the book a wrong move? Tarygin had clearly wanted the book published, not just recovered.

Krakin shook his head. "No deal. You made an agreement to buy the book and publish it. My client wants the money."

"Are you crazy?" Andrews said. "He's willing to give the

book back. Isn't that enough? If that thing is published, your client is going to wind up in jail or a labor camp. And you'll probably be with him."

"I have my job," Krakin said, "and I intend to do it."

"Krakin, be reasonable," Putney said. "Just take the book back. Polokov will be happy; he thinks it's gone. I'll be happy. And you'll be happy, because you'll stay out of jail or worse." As Putney spoke he pulled a brown leather satchel out from under his seat. He opened it and slowly removed a dog-eared, stained sheaf of papers, bound together in a brown cardboard cover. "Here it is. Your precious manuscript. Just take it."

Krakin took the proffered papers in his hands. He started to thumb through them quickly. This was the manuscript, all right. He felt good again. But it wouldn't do to bring it back. It just wouldn't do. He began to hand it back to Putney when the plane shuddered. Krakin noticed that the whining sound he had been hearing since he entered the plane had become quite a lot louder. With the shuddering it increased again. Krakin stretched his neck and looked around Putney and out the window. To his amazement, the lights of the terminal building were slowly sliding by.

34

"We're moving!" Krakin said. He looked behind him. The plane was almost full now. "What the hell is going on?" he asked Andrews.

"I'm afraid, Mr. Krakin," Andrews said, "that I may have been wrong when I told you about the timing of the affair this evening. It appears that because of the snow the publishers have to leave now."

Too late Krakin realized why the reception in the meeting room had seemed to have more Russians than Westerners, why

Khrushchev had been standing near the entrance to the aircraft gates. They must have already been preparing to leave when he and Andrews arrived. "You son of a bitch, Andrews. Get this plane stopped." Krakin started to get out of his seat. "I'll stop it myself."

The big, familiar pistol appeared in Andrews' hand, shielded by his body from the passengers behind him. The barrel poked into Krakin's side. "You'd better just sit down, Krakin. I can kill you now. I'm on my way out of the country. When we arrive in the West I'll say you were a hijacker, or a stowaway, trying to get out of the country-- that you threatened us with a bomb or something. Everyone will believe that. You don't have any travel papers, you know."

"They won't let you leave the airport with me on board. They'll stop the plane and arrest you."

"Who will? Who knows who you are? I just introduced you as my assistant. For all the Russians here know, you're one of us. That little trick with the accent that you pulled with the Premier played right into our hands. I couldn't believe it when you did it."

The plane was going a little faster now. It turned away from the terminal and taxied out into the dark, snowy night.

"Come on, Andrews," Krakin said. "They must have checked for papers. They know I didn't have any."

Andrews shook his head. "Not on a VIP flight like this. They just count noses and match the number with the names on the passenger list." He paused. "And I took care of the list."

Krakin felt trapped. Should he try to rush the cockpit and stop the plane? Andrews might well shoot him. Not certain, but indeed possible. It wasn't worth the chance.

"You're not a man of your word, Andrews," Krakin said, trying to seem as unconcerned as possible.

"Surely you can't hold me to a promise I made under duress. You threatened to turn me in."

"If I go with you now, my letter will still be turned over to the KGB."

Andrews shrugged. "But I'll be out of the country. And I guarantee you my government isn't going to send me back to stand trial. You see, Krakin, I'm finished in this country, thanks to you. If I stay and remove you, there's your supposed letter to expose me. Yet if I stay and don't remove you, you're walking around out of control with information that might be used against me--whether voluntary or involuntary on your part. But at least I can take something along with me to appease my employer. Namely, you."

Krakin thought for a moment. "What about Miss Malchev?" he asked.

Andrews shrugged again. "You had your chance. I would have got her out with you. I'm afraid I can't do that any more."

Krakin's heart sank. He stared morosely out the window. There was nothing to see but blackness and the snowflakes that drove against the window and melted into tiny drops. He felt more than saw the plane reach the end of the runway and turn around. Andrews sat down across the aisle from Krakin, his gun still concealed next to his shoulder, still pointing at Krakin. Without any announcement-- Andrews had undoubtedly taken care of that--the engines roared and the plane accelerated, pushing Krakin back into his seat and causing the droplets to move in horizontal streaks across the window until they disappeared.

Krakin glimpsed the lights of the terminal below just before they climbed into the low clouds. He turned to Andrews, flushed in anger.

"You can't do this to me!" Krakin said intensely.

"I'm sorry. I really am. But I have to do it. You've left me no alternative."

"You'll pay. Somehow you'll pay."

Andrews shrugged. "Perhaps, but I doubt it. And please don't think of trying anything. I'm a very good shot, as I've told you. No one would doubt that you're a hijacker if I kill you now."

Krakin changed his tack. "What do you want me for, anyway? It doesn't help you to take me out with you."

"Krakin, you've managed to destroy my usefulness in your country. That's a major setback. My employer won't like it, not at all. I have a sneaking suspicion from the way you evaded my questions

this afternoon that you just may have some helpful information--
something to appease them with. I've been in this business long
enough to develop an instinct about who knows things, and my
instinct says you know a lot."

Krakin didn't bother to protest. It wouldn't have made any
difference. He just tried to look exasperated.

"Besides, Krakin," Andrews continued, "I kind of like you. I
want you to see the United States, to give it a chance. I think you'll be
happy you came." He stopped, realizing he had touched a nerve.
"Look, I'll see if I can do anything about getting your girlfriend out.
I can't promise that we will, but there's a chance."

Krakin stared at Andrews a moment longer, then threw
himself back into his seat in frustration and despair. Out of the corner
of his eye he saw Putney looking at him. He turned toward the bald
man, who quickly looked away, a smug, superior expression on his
face. Krakin stared at the ceiling, then at the blackness outside the
window. The plane was still climbing, away from Basilgrad, away
from Russia, away from Anya. Krakin shook his head, trying to
escape the feeling of loss. To occupy his thoughts he picked up
Polokov's manuscript, which he had placed on his lap, and thumbed
idly through the document that had apparently removed him from the
life he knew. The plane continued to climb.

35

They had reached cruising altitude and been flying level,
above the snow, for over an hour. Putney snored at Krakin's side. By
Krakin's calculation they were probably somewhere over the Baltic
since, Andrews had said, their destination was Paris. They had either
just left Soviet air space or were about to do so. All was lost.

Krakin dropped Polokov's manuscript onto the floor under his legs. He had read a fair portion of it and skimmed the rest. What irony, he thought. No wonder Putney wanted to return it rather than pay for it.

Krakin decided to remove his jacket and automatically began checking his pockets. His hand touched unfamiliar metal, and he pulled out Andrews' car keys. He looked across the aisle at Andrews, who looked back at him, not noticing the keys.

Krakin held the keys up. "Very clever of you," he said. "A nice touch. It really put me off my guard."

"A small sacrifice to make," Andrews replied. "My employer can afford it. Perhaps my replacement can even reclaim it."

Krakin tossed the keys at Andrews' face. Andrews let them hit his cheek and fall to the floor. His eyes remained on Krakin the whole time, his gun still pointed at Krakin's chest.

"Why don't you put that away? What can I do? We're out of Soviet air space by now."

"I think I'll wait a little longer, just to be sure."

Suddenly, without any warning, the plane banked sharply to the right and dropped. Krakin's stomach was in his mouth. There were exclamations from the passengers behind him.

"What the hell!" shouted Andrews. Krakin looked toward him. Andrews was sprawled across his seat and that next to it and was rubbing his head. The gun, however, was still in his hand.

A frightened hubbub arose in the cabin. "Look," someone shouted. "Out the left side."

Krakin scrambled to the window over the now-awake Putney, who was trying to orient himself after the sudden disruption of his sleep. Krakin saw at once what the shouting was about. A large contingent of the Soviet Air Force was flying in formation a few meters off the plane's wing tip. Krakin had never before found much enjoyment in his country's displays of military might, but this occasion made up for all the others. To his own surprise, he found himself whooping for joy.

"They've come for me," he shouted at Andrews and Putney. "I told you they wouldn't let you take me."

A voice came over a loudspeaker above Krakin's head, for the first time on the flight. "This is the pilot. Flight control has requested us to return to Basilgrad for a security check. We are agreeing to the request. Please remain in your seats. There is no danger, but our departure will be delayed for several hours."

The plane began another, slower bank around to the right. The noise behind Krakin had diminished to a rumble of complaints. Andrews sat across the aisle looking despondently at the gun, which was still in his hand. Slowly he slipped it into the holster under his coat. Putney, sitting next to Krakin, was fidgeting nervously. It pleased Krakin to see the publisher finally losing his aplomb.

"Cheer up, fellows," Krakin said brightly. "The pilot said you'll only be delayed for a few hours."

Putney glared at Krakin.

"Hey, don't worry," Krakin said. "I'm not going to turn you in for stealing Polokov's book. Not as long as you pay my client his money, that is."

Without a word Putney pulled a fat wallet out of his coat. He removed some bills and handed them to Krakin. I'm sure your client won't mind American currency."

Krakin counted the money. "The currency is fine, but I'm afraid we're going to insist on the official exchange rate."

Putney opened his mouth to speak, then closed it. He glanced toward Andrews, who said nothing. Putney removed some more bills from the wallet and gave them to Krakin.

"Thank you. It's a pleasure doing business with you." Krakin stuffed the bills into his jacket pocket. He handed the manuscript over to Putney, who took it with reluctance.

"How are you going to explain those?" Andrews asked.

"What?"

Andrews repeated the question. "The KGB isn't bringing you back because you're a hero, you know. You're a defector with a wad of American money in your pocket."

Krakin patted the jacket pocket nervously. Why did someone always have to spoil the fun? "You'll just have to tell them. You tried to kidnap me. You will tell them, too, because I can still send you to prison."

"Why should we? You think maybe we'd prefer to go to prison for kidnapping than for whatever else you might try to pin on us?"

Krakin picked up his jacket and pulled the money out of the pocket and looked at it. Should he trust Andrews to hold it for him? Would that do any good even if he could? The hell with it, he thought. He shoved the money back in the pocket and put the jacket on. Only one thing was going to get him out of this, and the money wouldn't make any difference. Besides, he had his job to do.

"Oh well," Andrews added. "It probably doesn't matter anyway. Our chances of getting down through that snow are even slimmer than the chance you'll ever see your girlfriend again if we do."

Krakin stared out the window. He could see stars above them in the clear, cold air. It was hard to believe that a blizzard was raging only a few thousand feet below.

36

The plane descended again into the blackness of the clouds and stayed in them for what seemed an interminable amount of time. Krakin looked at Putney's watch. As he calculated it, the time since they turned around was greater than the time before.

"Maybe they're taking us to a different airport," Krakin ventured.

"I doubt it," said Andrews. "Our welcoming party is in Basilgrad. They're willing to risk a landing in a snowstorm. After all, this is a Western plane with a Western crew and passengers, except for one defector."

For a moment Krakin thought he caught a glimpse of whiteness below, then nothing. Droplets of water were forming and being swept off the window again. Then suddenly they were out of the clouds. The sky was full of white, blowing snow. Krakin made out some points of light in the distance, but he couldn't tell what they were or how far away.

The plane shook and started abruptly to descend. Now Krakin could see a fence and two snow-roofed gray buildings. They were much closer to the ground than he had thought. They must be about to attempt a landing. Krakin held tightly to the arm of his seat. The plane dropped. Were they down yet? Krakin couldn't see anything out of the window. Suddenly the engines roared. Krakin was pushed back in his seat. Had they landed? No, the plane was climbing again.

"Can't find the damn runway," Andrews muttered. The passengers behind them were surprisingly quiet.

The plane gained altitude, banked and turned. Krakin was covered with sweat. No one spoke. The pilot had made no announcement, but everyone realized that there was trouble.

After endless minutes Krakin felt the plane descending again. He couldn't see any more than before. This time, however, there was no sudden ascent. They touched the ground with a jolt and bumped along it, slowing very gradually--too gradually. The engines roared in a braking action, but out his window Krakin could now see the lights of the terminal building rushing past at a terrific rate. They continued on and the jolting and bouncing grew worse. Finally, after an eternity, they bumped to a stop. Out the window Krakin could see the flashing lights atop the heavy trucks plowing out through the snow to meet them.

As Krakin climbed down from the plane on rubber legs he couldn't help noticing the snow-covered, three-meter metal fence that seemed to run around the perimeter of the airfield. The nose of the plane thrust well over it, and the top of the fence stood less than five meters from the plane's front wheels.

37

Krakin found himself sitting on a hard wooden chair in a cramped office on the upper floor of the terminal building. He had left Andrews and the publishers in the meeting room below. God knows what they're saying down there, Krakin thought. But he had a bit of a problem himself. He looked across the table into the cold eyes of his old friend Varkov.

Varkov smiled. "You thought you were rid of me at Sverdlovsk, eh, Krakin? I've been watching you. I knew you were not a good citizen of the state. It was only a matter of time. The Army can't save you now." He spat on the floor.

"How did you know I was on the plane?"

"Very simple. One of our security men recognized you. When the plane left and you had disappeared, he informed me. He doesn't seem to like you very much either."

Krakin cringed. How could he have picked a KGB man to bait? What terrible luck. He had assumed that the man would contact Colonel Tarygin, if anyone. He forced himself not to reveal his discomfort.

"Well," Krakin said, "I am in your man's debt. If he hadn't recognized me, they would have succeeded."

"Succeeded?"

"Yes. They were trying to kidnap me. Thank God you stopped them."

Varkov stared at Krakin for a moment. Then he laughed loudly. "Kidnapped? Kidnapped? Yes, I would expect you to say that. A stupid thing to say, Krakin. Tell me, please, just precisely why they would kidnap you and then give you a large fortune in American money, such as this?" Varkov held up the roll of bills which had been removed from Krakin's jacket pocket when he was searched.

"Don't lose that, Varkov, or you'll be accountable for it. It's not my money."

"You were just holding it for the American agent, then? Perhaps it was too heavy for him?"

"I don't have to explain the money to you. I want to see Colonel Tarygin."

Varkov waved a protesting hand back and forth in front of him. "No. No. This is not a matter for the Army. This is a matter of internal security. I told you, the Army can't help you now, and I'm not going to invite them in to try. I made that mistake once with you. Now, there is essential information I must have before I can release the Westerners. Please tell me which of them were assisting in your defection. Was it the correspondent, Andrews? We know he's an agent. And you met with him in Leningrad. We know that. What were you trading to him for your defection? Information, most certainly. But what information? About Sverdlovsk?"

"You were the one who brought me to Sverdlovsk, remember? I was hardly spying."

Varkov banged the table with his fist. "Be quiet! I'll finish my questions, then you'll tell me everything. The alternative is considerable pain--more than you have ever imagined."

"You can't just keep those publishers waiting. They're very important in the West. You'll create an international incident. And for nothing. I don't have any information. Your head will roll long before mine."

"That most certainly is not true. Gregor!" Varkov called to one of his men who waited outside the door. The agent was inside the room in an instant. Varkov nodded toward Krakin, and Gregor calmly stepped behind Krakin's chair and twisted his arms backwards.

"Now, Comrade Krakin," Varkov continued. "Surely there is ground for my actions. Even if you were kidnapped, as you say, I must find the kidnappers. Correct? And the Westerners cannot object to the delay. They must wait until the snow stops and the runways are cleared before they can leave. And that may take some time."

"I warn you, Varkov, the Westerners must be allowed to leave, and I must be released. This is a sensitive matter that even you know nothing about. For your own sake, I suggest you check with Colonel Tarygin. Tell him about the money."

Varkov got out of his chair and stepped around the table in front of Krakin. He hit Krakin across the face with his meaty hand. It hurt. "You are ridiculous," Varkov said. "No one would make you a part of any matter of importance. You are nothing. An enemy of the state. A materialist. You care only for yourself, and your own pleasures. You tear down the foundations of our state, then you run away to sell us out to the decadent West." Varkov struck Krakin again, even harder. "Now tell me, who arranged for your defection?" Krakin was too groggy to answer even if he had wanted to.

There came the sound of muffled voices on the other side of the door. Or at least that was what Krakin thought he heard, over the ringing in his ears. Then someone came in. Two or three men, Krakin thought he saw through blurred eyes. Dressed in brown suits, all of them alike. And with high leather boots on which water (melted snow?) glistened. Or was that a trick of the light on the tears in Krakin's eyes?

"Well, well, Varkov," Krakin heard a voice say. "We meet again. And in the company of our old friend, Comrade Krakin. Would you please tell me what's going on here?" Krakin recognized the voice. Without a doubt it belonged to Colonel Tarygin. Krakin relaxed, and the hands holding his arms loosened their grip, awaiting developments.

Varkov told his story first, and Colonel Tarygin listened without expression. Then the colonel turned to Krakin.

"May I tell everything?" Krakin asked, glancing at Varkov and Gregor.

"I think Varkov and his men can be trusted, don't you?" Tarygin replied. The tone of his voice wasn't overly pleasant. Krakin tensed again.

"I finally determined," Krakin began, "that Putney, the publisher, had the manuscript. Tvori must have stolen it for him. So I came out here to get it. I forced Andrews to drive me. Putney was already on the plane, because of the snowstorm. I went aboard to see him. They tricked me into staying aboard until the plane took off. They were trying to kidnap me. They would have had me, too, if you hadn't sent out the Air Force."

"Air Force?"

"I called them out," said Varkov. "It was the only way to stop him."

"Good decision, Varkov," Tarygin said. Krakin didn't like the sound of that.

"On the way back," Krakin continued, "Putney agreed to pay me for the book, which he has with him. He gave me the money Varkov told you about."

"How much was it?" Tarygin asked Varkov.

"Twenty thousand American dollars."

"You see," Krakin said. "That's fifteen thousand rubles at the official exchange rate, which is exactly the amount Polokov agreed to sell his manuscript for."

Tarygin scratched his head thoughtfully. "Have you searched the Westerners?" he asked. "Or interrogated them?"

"Not yet," Varkov said.

Tarygin was sitting on the corner of the table, with his leg hanging over the edge. Then he stood up and straightened. "Well, don't. Let them go as soon as possible. All of them. I want them out of the country."

Varkov stared at Tarygin with his cold eyes. "I'm not in your command, Colonel. This isn't Sverdlovsk. You have no authority regarding defectors. I make my own decisions here. Even if this weasel is telling the truth, the Westerners attempted to abduct him. That must be investigated."

"There is far more to this than you know, Varkov. Release them."

"Never. That would be stupid."

Tarygin stared back at Varkov for a moment. Then he turned away and went to the door, which stood partly open. Krakin thought he saw movement on the other side. Was someone observing them?

Tarygin pushed the door open slowly to its full width. Two more men came into the room. Krakin gasped.

"Release them, Varkov," said Nikita Khrushchev.

Varkov gulped and turned pale. "Yes, sir, of course. I hadn't realized. . . ." He sank into a chair, his knees shaking violently under his baggy trousers.

"You haven't shown very good judgment in this, Varkov," the Premier added.

Varkov gulped again. "It's . . . it's very late, sir. I've had a hard day."

Khrushchev smiled a little. "Well, as Tarygin says, you don't know the whole story. I'm sure that with all the facts your decision would have been different."

"Oh, yes," said Varkov hastily.

The three men stood silently for a moment, ignoring Krakin, each appearing to be waiting for the others to speak.

"Well," Premier Khrushchev said finally, "I guess that completes it. Good job, Tarygin. Come on and have a drink with me." The Premier started to walk back out of the room. Tarygin followed him.

Wait, Krakin screamed to himself, what about me? Don't leave me with Varkov. But he didn't say anything.

"Oh, one thing, sir," Tarygin said. "What about this fellow Krakin?"

Khrushchev glanced in Krakin's direction. It wasn't a friendly look. "Varkov caught him. Leave him to Varkov."

Tarygin moved again to follow the Premier out of the room. Krakin's hopes fell as quickly as they had arisen. In the doorway Tarygin stopped again.

"The fellow was of some help to us. We wouldn't have known for certain what happened to the manuscript without him."

Krakin didn't hear any response and couldn't see the Premier any longer. Had he gone on? Did he even hear Tarygin's last words?

Tarygin shot a glance over toward Varkov. Varkov made a small gesture with his hand to Gregor. It seemed to be all he had strength for. But it was enough. The hands holding Krakin's arms released their grip.

Krakin stood up quickly as the footsteps receded down the hall outside the room. His arms ached fiercely as the circulation returned. But Krakin managed to raise his right hand. He stepped over to Varkov and offered it.

"Very nice to have seen you again, Comrade Varkov."

Varkov turned away. Through clenched teeth he muttered, "There'll be another time, Krakin. I'll have you sooner or later."

Krakin moved back to the chair where he'd been sitting. He patted Gregor's close-cropped head, then spun around, swept the roll of bills off the table and into his pocket, and followed the footsteps down the hall.

38

"I assume you were the ones who alerted Colonel Tarygin that I was headed for the airport." Kirus and Togorny looked at each other and then back to Krakin, who had asked the question. "Oh, hell, you don't have to tell me. Go ahead and pretend you don't know anything. It had to be you."

They were sitting in Polokov's office, waiting for the professor to arrive. It was late on Sunday morning. Krakin had had only about two hours' sleep, but he was anxious to get this matter disposed of. He didn't like sitting around with twenty thousand dollars in his pocket, especially when the money belonged to someone else.

"Anyway," Krakin said, "I suppose I ought to thank you. I don't like informers, and I don't like you in particular, and I'm sure you didn't call the Colonel to protect me, but there it is and I thank you."

Neither Kirus nor Togorny spoke. They just sat there and

stared back at Krakin. Finally Kirus said, with a tightly controlled blank expression, "We don't know what you're talking about, of course."

"Yeah. Sure." Krakin looked at the clock on Polokov's desk. "You sure he's coming?"

"He said he'd be here as soon as he can," Togorny answered. "He's in the middle of preparing an experiment. If you don't like waiting for people, you should let them know you're coming, instead of just barging in."

"Well, you'd think he'd be fairly interested in what I have to tell him."

"He probably assumes you're bringing bad news. Are you?"

Krakin laughed. "You sure play it dumb, don't you? Or maybe the Colonel didn't bother to tell you."

Krakin heard footsteps in the corridor. He went to the door and looked out. Polokov was striding briskly toward him.

"Well, Krakin, what is it?" Polokov said. "I'm very busy." He brushed by Krakin and went into the office. "If you've come for more money, save your breath. You've failed, in case you didn't know. I should have known better than to rely on someone like you."

Krakin looked toward Kirus and Togorny. "You may not want them around while we discuss this."

Polokov looked questioningly at Krakin. "I can't see what difference it makes, but very well. Go on and wait for me in the lab," he said to the two students. They left the room.

"Good luck in your studies," Krakin said as they passed him. "But remember to take time off to have a little fun once in a while." Krakin closed the door after them.

"Well, Krakin, out with it." Polokov acted very impatient.

"What makes you think I've failed, Professor?"

"The publishers are gone, aren't they? They left last night. And you never found the book."

Krakin took his wallet out of his pocket and removed the money. He slapped it down on Pololcov's desk. "I not only found your book, I sold it to Putney for you."

Polokov stared at the money. He picked it up gingerly and counted it. "This is American money," he said.

"Putney is an American publisher."

"But what am I supposed to do with this? I can't spend it."

"You can take it to the government bank and they'll be extremely happy to give you fifteen thousand rubles for it, or if you don't mind taking a little risk, you can get at least thirty thousand rubles for it on the black market. I'll leave that up to you."

"You sold the book to Putney, then?"

"I did."

"He will publish it?"

Krakin shrugged. "He bought it, didn't he?"

"But he told you he would publish it?" Polokov was even more intense.

"Look, I thought you had an agreement. Did he tell you he would publish it?"

"I never met him, just his messenger. I had no guarantee of publication. Why didn't you get one from him?"

Krakin looked at Polokov in disgust. He was incensed at the man's unbelievable lack of gratitude. "Look, Professor, how the hell do you get a contract to publish an illegal book from a Western publisher? Just tell me that, would you? God damn it, I got the money for you, didn't I?"

Polokov picked up the bills again and thumbed through them absently. "Yes, you got the money. But what good is the money? The important thing is that the world must know of my work." He stuffed the bills into his coat pocket.

Krakin watched the money disappear. "Professor," he said, "seeing as how that money isn't so important to you, surely you wouldn't mind paying me for my work."

"I thought I had."

"You gave me an advance. I told you I charge a hundred rubles a day, plus expenses. I'll settle for another five hundred."

Polokov looked at his desk thoughtfully. Then he reached in his pocket. "Here's two hundred fifty. You didn't get any contract for me."

Krakin took the money. Then he sat down.

"Well, Krakin, I assume that completes our business. If you don't mind, I'll get back to my laboratory."

"Sure thing, Professor." Polokov moved to the door. "Just one thing," Krakin continued. "If you'd like for me not to turn you in to the KGB, who will do very painful things to you before they send you away, and if you'd like me not to break your arms before I do that, I'd suggest that you pay me the rest of my fee."

39

The Sunday sun was gone, and so was most of the vodka in the bottle on the table next to the sofa in Krakin's apartment. Krakin and Anya huddled together on the sofa, but not to ward off the icy north wind that rattled through the dirty windows and guaranteed that yesterday's snow would last for a while. The vodka, and a bit of recent physical activity, had already taken care of the cold.

Anya ran her fingers slowly through Krakins black hair, a concerned expression on her face. "Leo," she finally said, "are you sure this Polokov matter is finished?"

"Reasonably sure."

'What does that mean?"

"It means I've finished my job, and I've been paid, and I'm off the hook with the KGB."

Anya frowned. "There are some things I still don't entirely understand."

"I'll bet you're going to tell me what they are."

"The first thing is, why would the American publisher . . . what's his name?"

"Putney."

"Yes. Putney. Why would he have the manuscript stolen when he was able to buy it?"

"Why not? It saved him fifteen thousand rubles. Who was going to turn him in? And who was going to catch him even if he was turned in? The safest theft in the world is from another criminal who can't do anything about it."

"But Putney is a business leader, not a common thief."

"They say that in the West there's not much difference."

"Is that why you didn't want to defect?"

Krakin thought. "I don't know."

"Did Andrews really offer to let you take me with you?"

"Yes. Did you want to go?"

"I want to be where you are. I don't care where that is."

"Well, would you rather be with me where you can have an automobile, and a refrigerator, and lots of jewels and no KGB?"

Anya laughed. "If that's the way it is in the United States, why didn't you accept? I've never known you to refuse a luxury or two."

Krakin's face went serious. "I don't know, Anya. I really don't know. I've learned how to survive here. Maybe what I've learned wouldn't be useful in America."

Anya stared at the coals glowing in the small fireplace on the opposite wall. "Your Professor Polokov wasn't very grateful, was he? And after all that work."

"Nope, he wasn't. He seemed to think I should have got him a guarantee of publication. Or maybe that was just a dodge to get me to take a smaller fee."

"Some people are real assholes."

"Not just an asshole. A clueless asshole. Polokov doesn't realize that publication of the manuscript would result in the end of his career."

"What do you mean?"

"If that book is published, Polokov will be on trial inside a month. To make an example of him, the government will say. First page treatment in the *Red Banner* for a week."

"I don't understand. Why did the Army practically beg you to sell the book for him if it was such a terrible thing?"

"Because they *want* to make an example of Polokov."

"Then why don't they just arrest him anyway. They've never needed grounds before."

"Won't work. Won't get enough attention."

"They can give it all the press they want."

"Here, yes. But not in the West. You see, the attention they want is the attention of the West. And nobody in the West knows about Polokov--yet."

"And *that's* why the Army wants the book published first."

"You got it."

"Oh, Leo, you're so brilliant." Anya leaned over and kissed Krakin on the lips. He reached for her but she moved back quickly out of his grasp.

"Just one little thing I still don't quite follow," Anya went on. She looked directly at Krakin. "Why in the world would the Army want the West to take an interest in Polokov's prosecution? That's just dumb. I mean, wouldn't sending scientists to prison for their research make us look foolish in the West?"

Krakin got up and began walking slowly around the room. "Now you're getting into the muddy part of it." He looked out the window. "I've got some pretty good ideas, though." He continued to gaze thoughtfully into the gathering darkness.

"Well?"

Krakin returned to the sofa. "I think it's most probably because the Army knows that Polokov is right."

"Polokov is right? Now that's really crazy. They want to convict a man for his ideas because he's right?"

"You see . . ."

"No." Anya put her hand over Krakin's mouth. "Don't tell me. I can figure things out too. Let's see, if the Army knows Polokov's theories are right, and yet they want to make a big show to the West of prosecuting him for those ideas, then they must want the West to think that they think that Polokov is wrong. Right?"

"Sounds logical to me."

Anya smiled proudly. "But why would they want to do that?"

Krakin refilled the two glasses on the table. There were a few drops left in the bottle. He poured them down his throat, then set the bottle on the floor and wiped his mouth with the back of his hand.

"Now," Krakin said, "we're coming to the real speculation. But knowing a little about Polokov's theories--and Lysenko's--we can make some educated guesses. As you know, the conventional wisdom--the Lysenko doctrine--is that environment controls not only development, but also heredity. Polokov, on the other hand, says that environment doesn't have a damn thing to do with heredity. Polokov apparently goes along with Western ideas on genetics, at least to a point. So what we've got to look at is matters to which these theories have practical application."

"Plant breeding, obviously," said Anya, taking a drink from her glass. "But why would the Army be interested in plant breeding?"

"There are certain kinds of plants the Army is very much interested in. But they're not the kinds of plants a farmer grows. In fact, one doesn't usually think of them as plants at all."

"Algae?"

"Hmm. Actually, I was thinking of bacteria and viruses."

"Biological weapons!"

"You got it. I think it's likely that the whole Sverdlovsk complex is devoted to work on biological weapons."

"God, how horrible."

"This is speculation, of course. But if it's true, you can see why the Army would want very much for the West to think it was doing its research on the basis of invalid theories."

"But you said Lysenko is in charge of the operation. That must mean either he's changed his theories or he's been trying to mislead the West for his whole career. That's pretty hard to believe."

"That part bothers me, too. The only way I can explain it is that Lysenko is being duped, too. That's not inconceivable, considering what he told me about the way the project is being run. The only reason they've got him there is to maintain the deception. Poor fellow doesn't even realize what's going on."

"Leo, do you think Andrews suspected any of this?"

"I'm not sure. He's a smart cookie. He sensed I knew something. He wasn't engineering my 'defection' just because he liked me. Nor even to help him save his own skin. He didn't need to take me along when he walked away from this thing."

"Why did he shoot Tvori?"

"Who knows? Maybe at that time he just didn't want me to find out that Putney had the manuscript stolen. Maybe he wanted to implicate me in something. Maybe he was just shooting at me and missed."

Anya shivered. "Oh, that's scary, Leo." She took another sip of her drink, then leaned back on the sofa and closed her eyes. "I wish you wouldn't take on jobs like this. I can't stand it."

"Too dangerous?"

"No. Too complicated." They both laughed.

"Oh," Anya said, "I almost forgot. I got a letter from Karin." She picked up her purse and started to go through it.

"Is she all right? That's the part of this whole thing that I've really felt bad about."

"She says she's fine. She misses Basilgrad, but she's actually been promoted. It doesn't sound as though she's being punished."

"Good. I wouldn't be surprised if the Army's involvement has protected Karin. Sometimes I even get the feeling that the KGB is softening up a bit. What else does she say?"

"She says she's still expecting you to take us to the ballet. Other than that, I don't know." Anya held up the letter. There were more holes than there was paper. "The KGB censor has been busy." They both laughed again, but Anya stopped rather quickly.

"Is something the matter?" Krakin asked.

Anya looked into Krakin's eyes. "There's something that still bothers me. About your safety. I'm almost afraid to ask you."

"Please go ahead. There's nothing to worry about."

Anya hesitated, then spoke. "You told me what's going to happen to Polokov if the book is published. I want to know what's going to happen to you. Won't they accuse you right along with

Polokov? You helped him. He's sure to involve you."

"Yes, they probably will if the book is published." Anya looked suddenly very frightened. Krakin patted her cheek softly and kissed it. Then he went on hurriedly. "But you don't need to worry about that, because the book isn't going to be published."

Anya's expression changed from fright to confusion. "I don't understand. Putney worked so hard to get it. Are you sure?"

Krakin nodded. "I'm sure. Putney told me, on the plane, before we got back to Basilgrad. I spent a fair amount of time going through the manuscript, and I can understand his decision."

"Why isn't Putney going to publish?"

"Believe it or not, it's because of Polokov's ideas. Putney didn't realize until he got the book in his hands just how far Polokov's theories go. Polokov doesn't stop with putting down Lysenko's proposition that environment affects heredity. He goes on to show, he says, that the environment doesn't have much effect on anything else either."

"So?"

"Can't you see what that does to Western ideas of self-improvement and equal opportunity and all that? According to Polokov, the abilities of an organism, including a human, are determined the day the organism is conceived and damn little can be can be done to change them one way or another thereafter. And he purports to illustrate the point with statistics on differences in the achievements of various racial groups. Putney told me that if he published stuff like that, the American establishment would come down on him so hard he might have to go out of business. The racial implications go right up against Western ideology."

"That's sort of ironic, isn't it? Poor Polokov, his theories are so out of step he can't get them published anywhere, even if he's right. What kind of enlightened world do we live in, anyhow?"

"I don't feel sorry for that son of a bitch."

"I feel sorry for us, because of *our* stupid environment."

Someone knocked loudly on the door to Krakin's apartment. Anya stiffened and put her hand to her mouth. "Oh, God. Who can that be?"

Krakin felt a sharp twinge of apprehension. "Just calm down. I'm sure it's okay." He got up and tiptoed to the door, motioning Anya to be quiet. He put his ear next to the door and listened. The sound of heavy wheezing came from the other side. Krakin laughed. "Oh, hell. I'd forgotten what day it is." He opened the door and beckoned the short, fat man inside. "Hello, Comrade Walnik," Krakin said.

'Hello, Krakin. Hope I'm not too early. Hello, Comrade Malchev." Walnik leered at Anya.

"That's all right, Comrade Walnik. I've been so busy I'd forgotten that the writing group meets tonight. You've given me a few minutes advance notice."

Anya got up from the sofa and picked up the glasses. She headed for the kitchen. "I'll put on some tea," she said.

As soon as Anya was out of the room Walnik edged close to Krakin. "There's a reason I came early," he said in a hoarse whisper.

"Yes. I guess I know what it is."

Walnik removed a folded envelope from his coat pocket. "I received this letter just yesterday." He opened the envelope and took out a second, sealed envelope. "All that's here is a letter addressed to you. The outside envelope was postmarked in Leningrad." He handed it to Krakin.

"I was expecting this. Thank you." Krakin took the letter. He turned it over in his hand and examined it.

Walnik said nothing further and turned away from Krakin. Krakin smiled. "Well, what did you think of it?" Krakin asked.

Walnik turned back toward Krakin. His face turned a deep red. "Think of what, Krakin?"

"The letter. Obviously you read it, or you would be asking me questions about it."

Walnik swallowed. "I'm sorry, Krakin. I didn't think you'd notice."

"That's all right. It was addressed to you, wasn't it?"

"Is what you say in there true? About this American Andrews killing a Soviet citizen?"

"Just suspicions, Comrade Walnik. Something I came across in working on an article. I wanted my notes to be in safe hands, while I was working on the piece, and I couldn't think of anyone more reliable than you. It doesn't make any difference any more, though, because I've found out that this Andrews fellow has left the country, apparently for good."

"Gee, that's exciting, Krakin. I sure envy you."

"To tell you the truth, I'd just as soon not get involved in possible murders."

Walnik laughed. "I guess so," he said. His eyes turned to Anya as she came back into the room. "Still," he went on, looking at Anya, "I wish I knew a few Americans, with some influence."

"Why do you say that?"

"Well, just between you and me, Krakin, and I know you're not the sort to report people--besides, I've got a little something on you--just between you and me, I wouldn't mind getting out to the West, where a man can live his own life. And be pretty well off, besides."

"It has its attractions, all right."

Walnik finally returned his gaze to Krakin. "Don't you sometimes wish you had an opportunity to get out, Krakin? A man of your talents."

Krakin glanced at Anya before he answered. She gave him a knowing look. "Yes, I suppose I do, Comrade Walnik. I suppose I do."